MILLIONAIRE MISSING

James E. Ballou

Enjoy !

Jim Ballou

PUBLISH AMERICA

PublishAmerica
Baltimore

First printing

All characters in this book are fictitious, and any resemblance to real persons, living or dead, is coincidental.

PublishAmerica has allowed this work to remain exactly as the author intended, verbatim, without editorial input.

Hardcover 978-1-4560-3101-5
Softcover 978-1-4560-3100-8
PUBLISHED BY PUBLISHAMERICA, LLLP
www.publishamerica.com
Baltimore

Printed in the United States of America

The man watching with binoculars remained hidden, observing events with a silent concentration, mentally assessing the situation. At the other end of the park everything appeared normal, and people carried on as people normally do in a city park. Two teenage boys rolled by on their skateboards. A group of boys and girls were playing volleyball around a suspended net. Several hundred yards away a man repeatedly threw a Frisbee for his dog, and a family with two small children was setting a park table for a picnic in a grassy area under a huge tree.

A typical Sunday in the park, with sounds of laughter, voices in the distance, and an occasional dog bark punctuating the late morning. But something sinister was about to happen, and the man watching with binoculars continued observing, and waiting.

Before ten minutes had passed, a figure emerged from a cluster of hedges and made a fast dash toward the picnic area. The man of the family was some seventy yards away with his little boy, who needed to use the public facilities. The masked figure dressed in green tights scooped up the two-year old girl and sprinted across the grass toward the tree line on the opposite edge of the ball field, unhindered by the mother's screams or the shouts from other recreationers.

Several young men tried to chase down the kidnaper, but soon lost him in the wooded area. One of the volleyball players was already dialing 911 on her cell phone when the little girl appeared out of the trees, visibly frightened but apparently unharmed. And then the loud yelling could be heard from somewhere among the trees. The young men who'd given chase went to investigate.

They found the frustrated kidnaper dangling upside down at least six feet from the ground, hanging by a rope tightly wrapped around one of his ankles and secured high in a eucalyptus tree. He flailed his arms in anger and cursed, but it was obvious he wasn't able to loosen the knotted rope on his own. His mask dangled freely by its head strap, revealing his angry face. A half-hour later the police arrived, directed to the spot by the girl on her cell phone.

As it turned out, the kidnaper matched the description of a suspect in three other child abduction cases. But even with all the witnesses to this particular kidnapping attempt, nobody could explain how the perpetrator was caught, or who caught him. That remained a mystery, baffling police and reporters for a long, long time.

CHAPTER I

Things were predictably slow throughout most of the first week that Delmar Mackenzie's Professional Investigative Services was open for business. The office rent; two-month's plus deposit, directory advertising, investigator's license, office furniture, computer hardware including printer and scanner, copy machine, phone lines, and camera equipment all added together made for a larger expenditure than Del had initially planned on, and even with his savings and credit card limits, which he previously expected to be more than sufficient, he soon realized he barely had enough to get his agency off the ground. In many respects, this was a whole new experience for Del, who at forty-four years old had never owned and operated his own business before now.

He hadn't hired a secretary yet. He decided to wait a while before hiring anyone, at least until the phone was ringing more than just twice a week. Thus far he'd received no reasonable job offers, at least nothing he considered reasonable. His first call was from a young girl who actually wanted to employ him to find her missing dog. He politely declined, explaining that he had no experience finding lost animals.

It was much too early in this new venture to become discouraged he realized, and he felt confident that once he had some cases to work on, his life would start to pick up again. The business cards he ordered weren't even printed yet. He would have to wait two more days for them.

He couldn't stop thinking about the career he'd thrown away. He had been getting close to a promotion when he let his frustrations over a certain unsolved case influence his actions. Reflecting back on his twenty-one years with the Los Angeles Police Department, he thought about just how good things had really been for him. If only he had it to do over again—he couldn't get that thought out of his head. But there could be no going back. He'd burned his bridges behind him, and he knew it. He was the fool who walked away from a good thing. Now he would have to make it on his own.

It seemed like the logical thing to do, to start a private detective agency, with his background in law enforcement and criminal investigation. And he still had some friends on the force, who'd help him out he was certain, if he needed them. But running his own business would involve quite a bit more than that. He was just beginning to learn how much he really didn't know about running a business. He wasn't afraid of it, but he knew he'd have to adapt to a new way of life, with a whole different set of responsibilities. That was going to take some time.

Finally, at a few minutes after ten on Friday morning, he took a call from a woman who at first identified herself only as Wendy. She wanted to hire him to find her brother.

"I'm convinced nobody else is able to find him," she remarked.

"What makes you think I can find him, if nobody else can? I've only been a licensed private investigator for a week."

"Because I know how focused you can be on a job."

"How do you know that? What do you know about me?" he asked.

"I know you were one of L.A.P.D's finest, and I know you were making progress on my brother's case when you left."

"Okay. Now I know who you are. I thought your voice sounded familiar. You're Wendy Luppert, right? Look, lady, I lost a good career over that case, and I'm not really anxious to spend any more time on it. You'll have to find another investigator."

"But no one else knows the case like you do. Besides, you're the only real-life Sherlock Holmes I know of. I paid attention to the investigation, and I noticed how focused you were. I think 'obsessed' was the term used in some of the editorials in the paper. Don't you have any desire to finish what you started?" she pleaded.

"That whole deal got me locking horns with my boss. Cost me my career with the department."

"What I heard was that you quit the job. I was told nobody actually fired you."

"Sounds as if you could do your own investigating. I can't imagine any reason why you would need me."

"Because you've already worked on the case. You know more about it than anyone. I could help you with it, but I need you."

"I'm sorry, Miss Luppert, but I'm afraid I'll have to pass," he said with regret, knowing how much he needed the work, but also remembering how frustrated he became with the case prior to leaving the force.

"I'm willing to pay five-hundred a day, plus expenses. And you wouldn't have to deal with the politics of a police department," she offered as a last chance plea for help, "but maybe you have a bigger job in the works right now. If that's the case, then could you at least refer me to someone else who might be able to help me?"

"Did you say *five-hundred a day?*"

"Plus expenses," she added.

There was a pause while he reconsidered the offer.

"I'll need your full cooperation," he said finally, "and I'll have plenty of questions about Trevor, about his childhood, his personality quirks, and some of the things that only his sister is likely to know. I'll be putting together a new psychological profile. I had that much started when…Well, anyway. That's water under the bridge. But I will be asking for your help with it."

"I want to do whatever it takes to find my brother. Anything I can do to help the case, I'm willing to do."

"Good. For starters, if you've got an old photo album with any pictures of him, or any old letters he may have written, we might find something helpful in it."

"I've got some things to show you. How about meeting me at my apartment tonight, say around seven, for dinner? We can thumb through a pile of photographs, and see what we find," she offered.

"Why Miss Luppert, did you just invite me over on a date?"

"Call it what you want, but I just want to find my brother."

"What are you planning to cook?"

"Spaghetti, if you like spaghetti. It's my specialty."

"Love spaghetti. I'll bring some red wine."

Del had been to Wendy's apartment before, during the police investigation. But it had been early in the investigation, and their questions concerning Trevor Luppert had been the basic routine kinds of questions usually asked at that stage of a missing persons case. The police had plenty of photos of Trevor from other sources, so they never bothered to ask her for any. And although Del had planned to contact Wendy later for more information when he'd started his profile, he was off the case before he ever got around to it.

What he remembered about Wendy, more than anything else, was how pretty she was. She had long dark hair and a warm smile to complement her pretty looks, and Del had noticed that much. But the day he met her she seemed understandably worried about her missing brother. A quick glance inside her apartment revealed the domain of a tidy, independent woman. He guessed she was probably in her early thirties, and he noticed she wasn't wearing a ring. Nor did he see any framed pictures of loved ones adorning any of her walls or tabletops. His guess was that she had never been married. That probably had something to do with what he perceived as the independent nature of her personality. His thoughts soon shifted back to the subject of the visit, and he never got around to finding out more about her.

That was going to be different tonight. He would have his usual essential questions about the person he was hired to find, but he was determined to learn more about Wendy, now that the opportunity was presenting itself. She was something of a mystery to him at the moment.

The disappearance of her brother was certainly a strange thing. Trevor Luppert was the founder and president of Luppert Systems, a security and surveillance systems manufacturer well known for its innovative developments in the field of surveillance technology. The firm had made financial news headlines several times during the previous two years for the enviable government contracts it had secured, but was in the regular national news almost daily for nearly a month right after the disappearance of its famous founder and president.

And there were plenty of theories circulating on what actually happened to Trevor. Some speculated there was some kind of government plot to keep certain technologies secret. Others were suggesting he'd been kidnapped for ransom. His estimated net worth was somewhere between four and five hundred million dollars at the time of his disappearance, depending on the information source. Some reporters were questioning a supposed thirty million in cash that mysteriously showed missing from his known assets, *after* he had vanished. There was even a rumor going around that he had become disenchanted with the civilized world, and had quietly escaped to a remote island far away from anywhere. That particular theory seemed to grow the longest legs of all of them. He was known to be an eccentric.

Regardless of the improbability of some of the theories, the inescapable reality was that *something* had happened to him, and exactly what nobody seemed to know. Even the FBI seemed baffled.

Del was trying to decide exactly where he was going to begin. A high-profile case like this always exhausted a lot of leads quickly, because there were always a lot of other detectives to compete with. The Los Angeles Police Department had conducted its investigation, case still not closed. Federal agents had made their own investigation, because of who Trevor was, and the nature of his firm's products, and there were plenty of reporters doing their homework. The one advantage Del had over everyone else was Trevor's sister. Wendy wasn't talking much to reporters or federal agents apparently, but she was obviously more than willing to work closely with Del. He saw this as a big advantage in this type of a case.

When he arrived at her place she had the table set for two, and her apartment was filled with the aroma of tomato sauce. He uncorked the bottle he'd brought and filled the two wineglasses on the table while she retrieved the hot spaghetti dish from the kitchen.

There was an unmistakable romantic nuance to the atmosphere, and the two of them exchanged curious glances as they began to eat, before engaging in actual conversation. And when the dialog commenced it was centered on the search for Trevor, as was expected.

"I was able to find some old letters he had written to my mother before she died," explained Wendy, "and some photographs taken back in the early seventies, when Trev was pretty small. My mother saved things like that. When she died three years ago, I wound up with the box full of her sentimental keepsakes."

"Excellent. Those are the kinds of things I'm always interested in studying when I'm on a case like this. I've always maintained the opinion that the more we learn about the subject of a particular mystery, the better our chances of unraveling it. Seems like old-fashioned common sense to me. Sometimes it's those tiny, seemingly insignificant bits of information that get overlooked. And sometimes, not always, but sometimes they contain hidden clues."

She took a sip of wine and then smiled. She knew she'd hired the right investigator. And she liked Del. She liked everything she had observed about him. That had been the case the first day she set her eyes upon him.

After dinner they rummaged through the pile of photos and letters she'd dumped out onto the coffee table. There were baby pictures of Trevor and Wendy, and various other candid shots of them taken while they were growing up. Trevor was usually seen with little tape recorders or transistor radios, while Wendy had her dolls. Del studied them, hoping to find something of interest, but failed to see anything that caught his attention. It seemed as if there should be something in all of it he should make special note of, but he couldn't put his finger on it.

"Looks like your brother liked electronics as a kid," he remarked, in his mind assigning very little significance to that observation.

"Oh yeah, that was Trev. He *loved* electronics. He was always rigging up some strange gadget with wires and diodes and all that. Dad bought him a soldering iron when he was five, and that was the start of it all. If he wasn't reading paperbacks about spies and secret agents, he was wiring something together. And if it had to do with spying on people, the more he liked it.

"Once, while my folks were out to dinner with friends, Trevor took apart the telephone on the kitchen wall and installed a bug. Nobody knew he'd done it, and he was able to sit in his room and listen to entire conversations. When my Mother discovered his listening apparatus while cleaning his room, she and my Dad punished him by grounding him for two weeks. I think my Dad was secretly proud of him for his genius, but had to set a moral precedence. Trev was only eight years old when he did that. Grounding him wasn't really punishing him, though. Trevor spent most of his time in his room anyway."

"All that I've learned about your brother supports that genius description. Luppert Systems' products are known to be cutting edge in surveillance technology. I guess he invented a lot of those things himself, didn't he? It seems that's what most people believe, anyway."

"Yes, in fact he did. He spent almost thirty million on a special laboratory for test and research. A couple years ago at a barbecue I heard him telling someone that he'd secured just a few patents shy of a hundred. Trev might have been a lot of things, but an exaggerator he wasn't. While growing up he experimented with hundreds of circuit boards and weird contraptions. Everyone knew way back then that he was a true genius, and that he would grow up to be a prolific inventor."

"Well, he proved 'em all right," Del said, wondering how all of this information might somehow be useful. He stared at a picture of a youthful Trevor and wondered. There just *had* to be something there. He couldn't put his finger on it.

"If anybody *did* kidnap my brother, they would have to have their act together all right. There probably hasn't been much printed about spying, secret operations, lock picking, or prison escape that he hasn't read. He lived and breathed that stuff all the time he was growing up. And to keep himself physically fit, he's been training in several different styles of martial arts for the past…ten or fifteen years. I've always been confident that he could take care of himself."

"Yes," commented Del, "I do recall reading about his passion for kick boxing and that sort of thing. He was well known for that, I guess."

She nodded, "And he could afford the best trainers, when the company started doing well, I think beginning around 1993. He'd already been training a while before that, but he got a lot better after he got a personal trainer. He got pretty good."

"Tell me more about his personality. I know we discussed the subject briefly when I was here before, and I've read the biographical articles, interviewed some of his employees, but an investigator can never have too much information."

"Well," she said, "I lost track of how many times I've heard people call him eccentric. I suppose that in a lot of ways the description fits. He's more introverted than might be expected of someone in his position. And whenever he gets an idea to do something, he'll usually become totally obsessed with it. That's how he's been able to do a lot of what he's done—things most people wouldn't even attempt. But he focuses extremely well because of it. And like I said, he's really, really smart."

"Do people like him? I realize he has a lot of friends and he's certainly popular, but would you describe him as the likable type? Some people have friends because of their status or prosperity, even if they have difficult personalities."

She laughed, "Trev definitely isn't difficult to get along with. If anything, I'd say he's *too easy going*. He's the quiet type.

He's shy, but usually very polite. Maybe he's a bit eccentric, but not at all difficult. Anyone who says he doesn't like him just doesn't know him very well. But he doesn't have any really close friends that I know of. I don't think he ever did."

"Can you think of anyone at all who might hold any kind of grudge against him?"

She thought for a moment.

"Boy, that's really tough to say. I'm sure there are quite a few out there who are tortured with envy. My brother is a gifted individual. I suppose it's possible there could be someone who is jealous and angry, but I wouldn't have a clue who that would be," she raised her eyebrows, "I've run the possibility through my mind quite a bit, just as I have with every other possibility that's popped into my head since he disappeared. But nobody in particular comes to mind. I just can't see anyone actually wanting to harm Trevor. He doesn't make enemies like that."

Del listened to what she said without comment. She then rose to her feet and went to the kitchen, returning with the bottle of wine to refill their glasses. There were still some old letters to read, and more old photos to search through. Wendy had no desire to see Del leave just yet, and she knew he still had more questions. The night was still young.

The nervous delivery boy was escorted into the plush office of the boss by two of his henchmen. Mr. Malone sat in his high-back brown leather armchair behind the heavy oak desk, lighting a cigar as the men entered the room. One of them closed the door behind them.

There was an uncomfortable period of silence before he spoke. He seemed to be toying with his cigar more than actually smoking it, like a man who was bored. He appeared to be annoyed, but he finally looked up with a stone cold stare at the tense young man standing before his desk, and spoke with little expression.

"Eddy, Eddy, Eddy. I chose you to bring the deposit to me because...Do you know why I chose you?" his eyes returned to the cigar in his hand, and he seemed to be studying it closely.

Eddy nervously shook his head. Mr. Malone smiled wickedly, looking again up at Eddy.

"When I first met you I told myself now here is an honest kid. Here is a kid I can trust to pick up a briefcase for me, and he won't even think about looking inside, because he knows it doesn't belong to him. But when I open my briefcase, I don't find the deposit inside. I find it full of telephone directories.

"Eddy, my friend, I know you're an ambitious kid. I was an ambitious kid just like you thirty years ago," his eyes narrowed, and his words turned to ice, "but what was in that briefcase didn't belong to you, and it isn't polite to take something that doesn't belong to you. Since I'm a nice man..." he glanced over at one of his henchmen, "I'm a nice man, right Franco?"

"You're a nice man, Mr. Malone," echoed Franco.

"And because I'm such a nice man, I'm going to give you a chance to return to me what is mine."

"But Mr. Malone," responded Eddy in a desperate tone, almost choking on the lump in his throat, "I swear I never opened..."

His words of denial were interrupted by the loud rap of the boss's fist slamming down abruptly upon his desk. Mr. Malone had obviously lost his patience, signaling his displeasure in being robbed. Now he raised his voice.

"Do you take me for a fool, kid? Was it some kind of joke? As you can see, I'm not laughing. I've done business with Black Dragon for a long time, and he always makes his exact deposit, because he knows what's good for him. It would not be his style

to send me a briefcase full of phone books. You should have considered that," he said, flicking his fingers toward the door, directing them all to leave his office.

"After the two of you dispose of this dirt bag, search his apartment. Search his car. Pay a visit to everyone he knows, or whatever it takes, but find that deposit," the boss ordered his henchmen to Eddy's horror, "I don't want to see either of you again until you have my eight-hundred grand. You know what to do."

The kid tried again to speak in his own defense as he was ushered out of the office, but he couldn't seem to utter a word. His heart pounded like a hammer inside his chest, and he started feeling light-headed.

Franco and his sidekick escorted the trembling and noticeably perspiring youth to a limousine parked on the street in front of the office building. They were going to take a quiet drive, explained Franco, to give Eddy the opportunity to reveal the location of the money.

A man watched the three of them enter the limo from his van parked across the street. He turned on his laptop computer and a city map appeared on the screen. He flipped a switch on a strange-looking radio receiver, and a little red dot appeared on the computer map, indicating the position of the limousine. He turned on the van's ignition and waited for the limo to pull out into the flow of traffic, where he would track it. He adjusted the earplug in his right ear and turned up the volume on the voice receiver. He listened carefully to every word spoken inside the limousine, but he had a pretty good idea where they were going. He decided to take a shortcut he knew and get there first. He could keep an eye on the laptop to see if his guess was accurate.

Twenty minutes later the limo rolled by the loading docks in an abandoned industrial complex, past a number of neglected warehouses toward the 150-foot tower at the far perimeter of the property where it stopped, and the passengers stepped out. The man called Franco held a Beretta pistol with a silencer on the barrel pointed at Eddy.

"The last poor kid who cheated Mr. Malone climbed that tower and took a bad fall," he said. "Or, I could just shoot you right here, but that wouldn't be half as much fun. Are you sure you don't want to tell me where the money is, kid?"

Eddy tried to make a futile plea for his life, "I swear I never opened that briefcase, Franco. You gotta believe me. I don't know anything about the money. I swear it!"

"Well, I'm afraid that's too bad for you. Trying to convince me won't help you. You needed to convince the boss, but the boss wasn't convinced. So, now you've got to start climbing some stairs. Unless you'd rather I get the job done right here. It doesn't make much difference to me."

"Those options stink almost as bad as you do, Franco Spaghettio."

The voice came from the tower's lowest platform, roughly a dozen feet above the ground. Heads turned in the direction of the voice, but all that could be seen was the heavy rifle barrel steadied on the railing, topped with a telescopic sight, and a small portion of a man's head covered with a ski mask. Most of his body was well protected by the heavy steel railing.

"This semi-automatic match grade AR-10 holds ten rounds of .308. I always use armor piercing ammo, loaded a little extra hot, just in case a limousine has ballistic Kevlar in the shell," the man on the platform explained. "But the kid is telling you the truth. He doesn't know anything. And I would encourage you to let him go free unharmed. I rarely ever miss at this close a range."

"Who are you?" asked Franco, clearly bewildered.

"Not important who," explained the man, "but you can tell Malone that I'm a vigilante. Tell him I monitor every move he makes, and listen to all of his conversations. Tell him I'm willing *to stop taking money from him if he stops selling drugs to the kids on the streets. And if you leave the kid here unharmed, I'm willing to let you drive away safely, so you can give your boss my message."*

Franco nodded to Eddy, signaling that he was free to move out of harm's way, and then he and his sidekick climbed back inside the vehicle, and in another instant it sped away.

Del Mackenzie had accumulated a volume of information about Trevor Luppert, and he had read through all that he'd collected several times, searching for anything that might at least point him in a certain direction. But he could find nothing in any of it that would seem to answer the questions he needed answered. In a lot of ways he felt more confused about the case now than when he quit the police department.

He made a list of all the different theories he'd heard, and then began contemplating them one by one, trying to get some sense of the probability of each. By this time he felt he had a pretty accurate, if only general concept of Trevor's personality. But still no leads.

The remote island theory was a troubling one. If Trevor had indeed been hiding out on some tiny island somewhere, it could prove to be next to impossible to find him. There must be literally thousands of tiny islands around the world. It would take more than a lifetime to search them all, as well as a lot more resources than Del had available to him.

On the other hand, it would be pretty difficult to settle anywhere in the world without at least *someone* knowing. Eventually he would be forced to interact with other people for supplies, medical services, or whatever. The world was a more populated place now than at any time in the past. There weren't too many places where a human could exist without at least a good chance of being discovered by other humans. Eventually someone would go public with information. But Del also realized that could take a while, and he didn't have that much time. Wendy wanted to find her brother as soon as possible, and Del would be pressured to show results within a reasonable amount of time.

When he asked Wendy what she thought of the island theory, she seemed to dismiss it as inconsistent with her knowledge of her brother, in spite of her characterizing him as an independent loner. He wouldn't want to exist in that kind of isolation without purpose, she explained. Trevor was always very purpose driven. Inward, but often motivated by some cause bigger than himself. It was a strange combination perhaps. Del made a special note of that personality trait. It could prove to be of some significance at some point.

All possibilities would have to be explored, no matter how unlikely. Del understood from experience that often the most unlikely, unpredictable scenarios turn out to be reality. He'd seen plenty of examples of that. He would follow a process of elimination to solve this mystery. That had always been his most successful approach in the past. And anyway, he didn't have any leads to follow just yet.

CHAPTER II

Del arrived at Wendy's apartment at seven o'clock sharp. An early start was usual for him, anyway, but this case would consume as much of his daily schedule as he was able to invest, and that was currently nearly every hour of daylight and more.

Wendy didn't have a regular job. Trevor had set up a special Trust before he disappeared just to take care of her, and she certainly had no financial worries. She played around a little with photography, but nothing she did generated sufficient income to support her. She was able to devote most of her time to the search for Trevor as well, and she was convinced that the best use of her time would be assisting Del.

As they sipped coffee, he shared some of his thoughts with her, and asked more questions.

"You mentioned before that he had never been married. Did he ever date any girls you know of?"

"Not since he started Luppert Systems. He didn't have time. My brother was a workaholic. He was always attracted to girls, and often times I was pretty sure that he was more than a little bit interested in some of the girls he'd met. But he was always so busy, and he just didn't need anyone."

"I know he didn't have really close friends, as you explained, but was he close to anyone at all? I mean, besides you?"

She shook her head, "No one. My brother didn't want to be close to people. I've always thought of myself as pretty independent, but probably not so much if you compare my personality with my brother's."

"Trevor is older than you by what, five years?"

"Almost exactly five years. Only one month short of five," she confirmed.

"Was he protective of his baby sister?"

"Sometimes. Almost two years ago an attempt was made to kidnap me, but it didn't get far. I was never in any danger. But the whole episode had a huge effect on Trev. I guess he felt somehow responsible, because it was his financial success that motivated the attempt. After that, he seemed obsessed with crime prevention and home security," she laughed, "He was in the right line of work for that."

"I'm surprised your apartment isn't wired with alarm systems and security cameras," remarked Del.

"Oh, believe me, if Trev had his way it would. He became totally paranoid about me. I think he even hired a private detective to watch me, but I was never completely sure of it. I got real sick of the whole thing after awhile—I just wanted to be left alone. I can take care of myself."

Del's eyes scanned her apartment, "Somehow I believe you can," he said.

"Well, as I was saying, Trev was consumed with crime after that, and it really bothered him a lot that he couldn't do much about it, even with all of his money. For a short time he was making generous contributions to several law enforcement budgets, as I'm sure you're aware, but that didn't last long. He formed his opinion fairly quickly that the money wasn't being used effectively to fight crime."

"I can only say that I never saw any of the money," Del said, "but this information is potentially important. There might be some connection with his disappearance, although I'm not yet fitting the pieces of the puzzle together. My curiosity is definitely stirred."

Wendy looked at Del and smiled. As important as it was to her to find her brother, she also realized that she was enjoying Del's company. She couldn't stop herself from thinking beyond their current professional relationship to possibly something else at some point. And she had the sense that he was thinking the same thing.

"You don't have a secretary yet," she noted, changing the subject.

"And how would you know that?" he asked, slowly raising his coffee cup to his lips, "You haven't even seen my office."

"When I called your office Friday, no secretary answered your phone. You answered your own phone."

"Maybe my secretary was on the other line. A good detective thinks of every possibility."

"That's right," she said, "except that when I put a call in yesterday while you were out of your office, I got your message machine instead of a person. Of course, I suppose it's possible that you let her have Mondays off. But if I were making a bet, I'd bet that you don't have a secretary."

He grinned, "Too bad you're not looking for a job. I could sure use someone like you to help me with things."

Her face glowed with pride, "I just might take you up on the job offer one of these days, if the position is still open."

Things were somewhat in a state of chaos at Luppert Systems since Trevor vanished. He had a way of keeping the company organized, in part by channeling the talents of his employees. Without him, the laboratory had no more fresh concepts to experiment with, and in more ways than one the main ingredient of the successful recipe known as Luppert Systems was missing from the mix. He was the one who brought everyone together to form a working operation, and he provided the innovative inspiration. Keeping it running smoothly without him was now proving to be quite a challenge.

Walter Collier, the company's vise president, never imagined he would be in the position he currently found himself in. After a month and a half of keeping things together and running like business as usual without the founder, he started noticing cracks forming in the business foundation. The morale among employees had fallen noticeably. People inside and outside the company started raising questions about the company's future. And Walter, though an effective general manager, was not an inventor. Even if the company had enough products and contracts to keep it alive for many years, as Walter kept reminding everyone, the general perception that no new developments would be introduced by Luppert could only damage an otherwise promising future.

And then there was the issue of the log books that started raising a bit of concern. When Karen, Luppert's bookkeeper, brought a curious discrepancy to Walter's attention, he started looking for others, and became very troubled when he found some.

"I thought it odd that Mr. Luppert would sign the release for the total inventory on those TL-9 microphones, for that demo you guys prepared for the CIA back in June," Karen said, "How many units would be needed for a demonstration, anyway?"

"All depends," explained Walter, "but usually a dozen is more than adequate. I don't remember how many we took to that CIA demo, but it shouldn't have been more than twenty, max. Sometimes we bring more than we normally do, if we anticipate a larger than usual audience. How many did we have in our inventory in June?"

"Over four-hundred. Four twenty-one, to be exact. Log shows that many were released with Trevor Luppert's signature, for that demo meeting."

Walter looked stunned, "You've got to be kidding. I wonder what he was planning with that demo. I don't remember him giving them away as tokens of appreciation. And anyway, there weren't nearly that many CIA personnel attending. How many of the TL-9's have we sold to date?"

"Fourteen hundred and change, if I remember correctly. The CIA purchased the majority of those. I think we only sold a little over two hundred to the FBI. Just read that figure a few minutes ago, but I left the production book in my office. This is just the log book here. I'll run and grab it if you want the exact number."

"No, don't bother. But that's not bad, considering the price we're able to get for those. Of course, the TL-9 is the best wireless listening device available at the moment. It has the best range, clearest reception, and the smallest size. It's a great product. Well, so how many of those four hundred that he signed out were logged back in after the meeting?"

"That's the weirdest part about it," she said, "I couldn't find any record of them being logged back in. Not any of them. Those four hundred and twenty-one microphones are simply missing, according to our records, just like Mr. Luppert himself."

"Well that just doesn't make sense."

"I can't explain it. And I have to account for production and inventory somehow. But there's more."

"Let's have it," he said with a sigh, dreading more troubling information.

"Well, I overheard Andy talking to Michael about one of the directional sound magnifiers."

"The Model IV Selective Ear we market, you mean?"

"Exactly."

"What about it? What did they say about it? We've improved it a lot since earliest production, you know? Did they mention any problems with it?"

"Andy was asking Michael what Mr. Luppert wanted to use one for when he logged it out only a week before he disappeared."

"Maybe he just wanted to play around with it a bit to make sure it worked okay. He does that a lot with his inventions. Nothing strange about that."

"But he never logged it back in. I checked the log," she said, then paused, "I guess none of this would seem so strange if he hadn't disappeared. But think about it. We've got four hundred plus missing TL-9 microphones, a missing Selective Ear worth $3,250.00, and a missing boss. Some other items on our inventory list are also unaccounted for, if you want to look at it. It just seems like something other than a coincidence to me."

"What's your theory, then?"

"I'm a bookkeeper, Mr. Collier, not a detective. I'm supposed to figure numbers, but I don't understand these numbers. Something is odd. That's all I'm saying."

"We could let the police know about these discrepancies you've found, if you're convinced they're pertinent to Trevor's disappearance. Maybe they can connect the dots."

"Maybe," she said, closing the logbook on her lap, "but I thought I should bring it to someone's attention."

"Does anyone else know?"

"No. I haven't told anyone besides you. But I thought you should have that sort of information before anyone else."

"Thanks, Karen. I'd like you to look into this further, and bring me what you find before we take it to the police. I know they'll have plenty of questions for us. I'd like to be as prepared as possible," he leaned back in his chair behind his desk, looking up at the office ceiling, "I wonder what became of that police detective working on the case who resigned," he said.

"Officer Mackenzie. Yeah, I thought that was pretty crazy whatever happened there. I guess he quit right in the middle of the investigation."

"No doubt they're all frustrated. They don't seem to have any leads, or at least, none they're talking about. Oh Trevor, buddy, where the heck are you?" he sighed, "We really need him around here. I don't know how much longer I can keep the company together without him. Trevor *is* Luppert Systems. I think I'd like to have a talk with that Mackenzie, wherever he is, and maybe find out some of what he knows. He may not want to talk about the case, but then again, he might be interested in all this you've brought to my attention. About a month ago he and that other cop came by snooping around the shop, asking all the employees lots of questions as I remember. They lost a serious detective when he left."

He reached across his desk for the telephone directory, and started turning pages.

"Do you remember his first name?" he asked.

She thought for a moment, "It's Delmar, I'm pretty sure. Yeah, I'm sure that's it."

"I'll see how many Mackenzies are listed under D., Del, or Delmar," he said, searching in the M's.

Leo Malone jammed his smoldering cigar down into the ashtray on his desk, and jerked his fist over his head in a show of anger. Franco and his sidekick stood in front of the desk, receiving their scolding in timid silence. Two other armed men were also present to ensure enforcement of Malone's rules, as usual.

"I send two grown men to do a simple job for me, and what do they do? They return to my office with that job unfinished, and tell me some crazy story about a vigilante! What shall we do with the two of you? Who is this man who claims to be a vigilante? Please describe him for me."

"We couldn't see him, boss," explained Franco.

"He wore a ski mask," his sidekick added.

"A ski mask?" the boss had a sarcastic look, "I never heard of a ski mask that stopped bullets."

"We didn't have a clear shot at him. He kept behind a steel railing. Thick steel. I doubt that our nine millimeters would come close to punching through it. He had a scoped rifle on us. That's why he's not dead right now."

"And what about the money?"

"The vigilante said he took it. Said he'll stop taking money from you when…" Franco hesitated to say it. It sounded ridiculous to him.

Malone put his hand up to his ear, "I must be hard of hearing, Franco, because I didn't get that. Please speak up."

"When you 'stop selling drugs to the kids on the streets', was how he put it."

Malone laughed, and his laughter was echoed by his other hired gunmen in the office. Franco and his sidekick tried to laugh along with the rest of them, but inside they weren't laughing, and that was obvious by the look of fear in their eyes. The boss was a cruel man, and everyone who worked for him knew it.

"He also said that he monitors you all the time, and listens to your conversations."

Malone's expression changed suddenly to serious. He contemplated Franco's statement for an instant, then reached across his desk for the telephone, immediately disassembling the handset. When his eyes noticed the tiny listening device his temper heated up, and he smashed it on his desk with the bottom of his ashtray. The others in the room were given to imagine a personality like Adolf Hitler in a bad mood.

"I want this 'vigilante' found, and brought to my office! Tony, I want you and Mario working on it. Maybe you'll have better success than these two incompetent losers taking up space in *front of my desk. I'll leave their fate in your hands. But I want this joker who's been stealing from me. Whatever it takes, I want to know who he is, why he's doing this, and how he was able to get into my office to plant this bug. I want you to make sure there are no other ears around here,"* he shook his head, *"I could get better office security on a school playground! I want some answers, and I want things taken care of right this time."*

Wendy was vacuuming her apartment when the phone rang. She almost didn't hear it, but when she finally did, she turned off her vacuum cleaner and rushed to answer it. Just as she hoped, it was Del.

"Do you have anything yet?" she was clearly anxious for any shred of news about Trevor.

"Maybe something. This afternoon I heard about something Trevor apparently did just before he vanished. I'm sure you'll find it interesting, as I did."

"I'm listening," she said, "let's hear it."

"I'll tell you over dinner. I know a good restaurant I think you'll like. Can you be ready in an hour?"

"No problem. But can't you give me any clues now? An hour is a long time to wait."

"Well, what I heard might explain some things. It might be a clue that at least he is likely still alive."

"I've expected that all along. But what is the clue?"

"It will take a little while to explain it properly. I'm hungry. I'd like to tell you all about it, over dinner. I'll see you in an hour."

"I'll be ready."

An hour and a half later they were seated at a table in a nice restaurant reading the menus while he explained the telephone conversation he had earlier with Walter Collier.

"I was surprised to hear from him," he explained, "but what he had to say surprised me even more. It appears that your brother disappeared with a whole lot of surveillance gear."

She thought about it for a moment, "So, what do you think it means?"

"May not mean anything. But it *could* mean something. It could be a clue that his disappearance was premeditated."

"You think he's hiding somewhere?" she asked curiously.

"It's a possibility that he's avoiding contact with other people."

She looked confused, "But I don't understand why. What would be his purpose? Or haven't you arrived at that yet?"

"I'm still working on it. Was kind of hoping you could help me with that, since nobody knew your brother as well as you did."

He closed his menu, finally deciding what he wanted to order, "I never asked you something, because I pretty much took it for granted that I knew the answer. But, has your brother contacted you at any point since his 'disappearance'?"

She looked surprised by the question, "No. But it's an odd question. If I had been in contact with my brother, why would I hire you to find him?"

"You're right. It wouldn't make any sense. Just making sure I ask all the questions, that's all. Have you decided what you're going to order yet?"

She shifted her attention back to the menu.

The waiter interrupted their binding stare a full minute after they laid down their menus, asking them if they were ready to order. At that very moment they both realized that their attraction to each other was a mutual feeling, and it was almost as if the ice had finally been broken between them. The balance of the evening turned out to be a much more romantic night than either had expected. Not much more was said about Trevor until the next morning when they woke up together at Del's place, and the subject came up while they were eating the scrambled eggs and bacon he fixed for breakfast.

"If we could figure out what your brother needed all that equipment for, we might have a clue as to what happened to him. That was quite a list of gear his company's vice president described to me. It has to mean something, as I see it."

"Did he seem to have any theories?"

Del shook his head as he finished chewing a bite of food, "If he did, he was sure careful not to specifically explain them. But he definitely knows something is up with it. It has something to do with Trevor's disappearance. The trick will be figuring out exactly what."

"That's why I hired you. But you know what?" she started to smile.

He shook his head, chewing another bite.

"I'm glad I did," she said.

Two men pulled nylon stockings over their heads just outside the bank, then drew their weapons from under their jackets and entered the building shouting commands and waving their pistols threateningly at everyone inside.

The two men immediately ordered the bank tellers to move away from their work stations to prevent them from activating any alarms. Demands for cash were made with a gun held to the head of one of the employees for persuasive intimidation.

Within five minutes the bank robbers exited the building with bags of cash and hurried into the back seat of the getaway car, anxious for a swift escape. They removed their hoods.

The vehicle's engine had been kept running and ready, but the two men fast realized that their driver wasn't in the driver's seat. A quick survey in all directions revealed nothing, except that the driver was simply missing.

"What happened to Willie?" one of them cried with panic.

"He probably got scared and baled," answered the other, "but I don't plan on sitting here waiting around for him."

He got out of the back seat and climbed into the driver's seat, quickly shifting gears into reverse and stomping on the gas pedal.

The vehicle's tires screeched over the blacktop and the car jetted backwards across the parking lot, until the slack was taken up in the steel cable that had been hooked to the front bumper and secured to a concrete light post at its opposite end. The sound of clanging metal followed as the bumper separated from the car body and bounced a few times on the parking lot, with the car's front license plate attached to it.

In their hasty departure, the bank robbers didn't stop to recover their bumper, or even attempt to investigate what happened. They just sped out of the lot in a desperate effort to get away.

Police sirens grew louder as they approached from multiple directions, and a second later their flashing lights could be seen in the traffic. The vehicle speeding away like a bat out of hell caught the attention of at least two units, and a chase ensued.

The original getaway driver was suddenly untied after his gag was removed where he had been bound and silenced just moments before in the hedge of arborvitae trees less than two hundred feet from the west side of the bank.

"Go turn yourself in, and participate in bank robberies no more," said the man whose face was hidden behind a mask, "I'll watch you from here, ready to pull the trigger if I see you try to bolt. And don't think I won't—I told you what I think of bank robbers."

"Who are you?" the bewildered getaway driver asked.

"A vigilante," answered the man wearing the mask. *He raised his rifle to his shoulder as if to take aim, "You better hurry up and turn yourself in before I start getting an itchy trigger finger."*

The man emerged from the hedges with his hands in the air as he approached a swarm of police in the bank's parking lot. The masked man watched them order him down onto the pavement and cuff his hands behind his back. The last thing the masked man observed before he quietly vanished from the area was the man on the ground nodding in his direction, obviously trying to alert the police to his presence. Two officers eventually searched the hedges, but they were too late to find anything.

Trevor's van had over two million dollars worth of high-tech surveillance electronics and computer gear mounted inside, well hidden from outside view. From this mobile station he could spy on just about anyone, anywhere, and at any time. He could monitor numerous radio frequencies simultaneously, record conversations, tap into phone lines, unscramble encoded communications, hack into computers, listen to individuals talking or even whispering in a noisy crowd from several hundred yards away, and a whole lot more.

Installed in the roof of the vehicle was a well-disguised compact periscope, with a night vision capable optic, having a high magnification zoom lens for accurate long-range observation, and a button-activated laser range finding system for precision distance calculation.

He'd spent almost two-hundred and seventy thousand on the van itself, making it ninety percent bullet proof against small arms fire, variable suspension system and all-wheel drive for on-road/off-road travel, tinted glass for maximum privacy, high-performance custom engine capable of sustaining speeds in excess of 120 m.p.h. for lengthy periods without overheating, with a fuel efficiency of around 45 highway miles to the gallon. He had an auxiliary thirty-gallon fuel tank installed, which was protected by a thick outer shell of rubberized synthetic for shock resistance, as was the main tank. Tires were filled with a special cushion foam to prevent deflation if punctured. The vehicle was equipped with the latest GPS navigational system, and an elaborate alarm system patented by Luppert Systems.

He registered the vehicle under one of his aliases to protect his anonymity. He carried identification and was licensed, rented an apartment, maintained bank accounts, and had insurance papers, tax documents, etc., to support his newly assumed identity. This had taken him some time to build. But his methodical planning and thorough preparations paid off, as he was able to survive and operate without leaving any traces leading to Trevor Luppert.

Just as his sister had described him, Trevor was a man driven with purpose, and his purpose, his *obsession,* was fighting crime. He was smart enough, and possessed sufficient resources to pursue his objectives more effectively than could be accomplished via the more conventional means of law enforcement, and his awareness of that fact instilled in him a sense of duty.

When he set out to monitor the criminal world, and to become involved with its endless problems, he considered the risks and sacrifices he would have to undertake. He'd spent a lot of time contemplating such things. But he knew he had to follow the path he ultimately chose. Follow it without looking back. For him there was no other way.

He'd been conducting his own investigations for quite awhile, collecting information about criminals and criminal activity through a variety of sources, and learning who to spy on, and when to spy on them. He had the tools and technology to effectively eavesdrop on those individuals he'd learned about, and he monitored his subjects with hundreds of bugs planted in strategic locations for listening, and with dozens of hidden video cameras positioned where they could view a good deal of activity. He even went so far as to dress himself in filthy worn clothes and dwell under bridges and in alley ways with homeless vagrants, to learn from them anything they could tell him about who was supplying drugs, etc. He had essentially created what he liked to think of as his own information "farm", and his full-time clandestine operations began when he decided that the harvest was ripe. By then he had eyes and ears seemingly everywhere around Los Angeles.

CHAPTER III

Leo Malone grabbed the remote control off his desk and pointed it at the television screen, pressing the power button to turn it off. He'd heard all the news he cared to hear for now. There was the report about the bank robbers who were caught by police with some help from an unidentified "vigilante". It was enough to get the boss's attention.

He called some of his hired men into his office for a meeting.

"Anybody watch the news this morning?" he asked.

Nobody nodded. They waited for him to expound.

"They're talking about this vigilante character out there in the city, playing God. They don't know who he is yet, but why should they? We haven't figured that out, either. He finds a way into my office and installs a bug in my phone, spies on me, steals my revenues, interferes with my business, and we don't even have a name! So I have to ask, *what sort of help have I hired?*"

"We're working on some leads, Mr. Malone. We'll get this guy, it's only a matter of time."

"How much time? Meanwhile he's free to make all kinds of trouble for me. The sort of trouble I really don't need. Tell me about the leads you have."

"Well, Boss, someone's been nosing around—asking a lot of suspicious questions on the streets. They're the kinds of questions cops ask."

"Same kinds of questions we'd expect this vigilante to be asking," added one of the others in the office, "about our street venders. We're confident that our information sources will lead us to this guy. We will have him for you very soon, Mr. Malone."

Malone lit a cigar and took a drag, then puffed a smoke doughnut that slowly drifted upwards over his desk, "Let's hope so. If this isn't done very soon, there will be consequences. *Huge* consequences."

Trevor had been tracking a serial rapist suspect for weeks. The year before, police detectives had done the same thing, and when they believed they had what they needed on him, he was arrested and his case went to court.

It had been a profusely reported ordeal, but to the astonishment of the public, the case was thrown out on a technicality. The man was released back into society a free man, and not much was reported about his life or whereabouts after several months had gone by. It appeared that everyone more or less assumed that he was being closely watched by authorities when in fact nobody was watching him. The top ranking members inside the police department were still feeling their embarrassment after the widely publicized failures of the first investigation, and they weren't eager to repeat the process. Besides, an indefinite round-the-clock surveillance of one man considered innocent in the eyes of the law was not a particularly easy to justify use of resources.

When Trevor learned that nobody was watching the man, he began his own surveillance operations. He watched him for a few weeks and learned his routines. While the man was spending his daily hour swimming at a local indoor pool, Trevor was in the man's apartment installing bugs and cameras. Without being detected in the dark of night, he mounted a tracking beacon under the man's car. These were the kinds of clandestine activities Trevor could never seem to get enough of, and he monitored the suspect closely for most of three weeks without raising any suspicion at all. But he hadn't observed anything terribly unusual.

And then the suspect's alarm clock beeped loudly. It was 2:30 a.m., and it sounded loud enough to wake Trevor up through the hidden microphone. He'd been sleeping in his van, which he had parked within telescope viewing range of the suspect's apartment.

The suspect had set his alarm for that time of morning for a reason, and Trevor was determined to find out exactly what the man was up to. He wiped the sleep out of his eyes and sat up on the floor of his van. The suspect was active, so it was time to get to work.

Fifteen minutes later he watched through his periscope with the infrared turned on as the suspect stepped out from his apartment and into his car. Trevor switched on the tracking screen, and then started the van's engine. He sat in the driver's seat and waited for the suspect's car to move.

A moment later the man backed out of his space under the apartment's carport and sped away down the road. Trevor waited a full minute before following him, so as to stay outside the man's field of view. After experiencing so much media and law enforcement attention recently, the man was likely extra suspicious of any people or vehicles around that could be there just for the purpose of watching him. Trevor knew he'd have to be especially careful in that regard.

He followed the man to the parking lot of a 24-hour supermarket and parked about three hundred yards away on a side street to avoid being spotted by him. It didn't take long to find the man's car with the periscope. He had already lit a cigarette, which appeared as bright as a flare through the night vision optic. The man was sitting there in his car obviously waiting for something. Trevor thought he had a pretty good idea what it was, but he patiently waited and watched. He didn't want to move up too close, not just yet, anyway. He waited to see what the man was going to do.

Just as expected, a young woman still wearing her supermarket employee's uniform exited the building and walked toward her car parked at the far end of the parking lot, next to several other parked cars apparently belonging to other night shift employees. She must have just clocked out at the end of her shift.

Before she reached her car, the man's car rolled between it and her and stopped right there. He rolled down his driver's side window as if intending to ask her a question, and she stopped, uncertain as to what she should do. He said something to her that Trevor wasn't able to hear, and then his car door flew open and he jumped out with a huge knife that reflected the overhead parking lot light.

This all happened so fast that Trevor didn't have time to get there and stop it, and he hadn't come up with a good plan to prevent it. The young woman was obviously caught by surprise, and before she could run away, the man had a hold of her arm, and his knife was at her throat for intimidation.

Trevor had to make a split-second decision. He wasn't sure whether the man intended to rape her there, in the parking lot or nearby, or pitch her into his car and drive to a different location. Nobody else was around at that time of morning to witness or interfere with the man's wickedness. Whatever might be done to stop it, if anything at all, would have to be done by Trevor, and it would have to be done rather quickly. The situation was mighty urgent.

He decided to stay with his van, with the motor running and ready to roll, and monitor the situation closely until he knew for certain. If the man drove away with the girl, he'd want to be following in his van, rather than be a couple hundred yards from his wheels on foot, closer to where the abduction occurred. His biggest fear was that the crazy son-of-a-bitch might cut her with that knife before he could stop him. From three-hundred yards it wouldn't be too difficult to knock him off with that scoped .308 semi-auto rifle he had, except that the rapist was too close to the girl, and there was too much movement at the scene for a clear shot. As it turned out, there wouldn't have been a shot, anyway. He forced her into his car and took off in another instant. Likely nobody heard her screams besides her attacker and Trevor.

Now he needed to rely on his technology like never before, as his only way of tracking the rapist now was with that tracking beacon, and the little glowing dot on the tracking screen. If he followed within visual range, he would run the risk of being noticed, and this situation was too dangerous for the victim to allow that. He knew he needed to keep at least four city blocks between them all the way.

Suddenly, while he was driving and monitoring the tracking screen both at the same time, he glanced down at the screen just as it started fading out. He watched with horror as the dot disappeared. Being at least four blocks away, he understood how easy it would be to lose the car, even with the small amount of traffic that early in the morning.

The only thing he could do now was hurry to the last known position of the car and hope to be able to spot it. He stepped on the gas to get there as soon as possible, without the aid of the screen map, and four blocks later his eyes hunted in earnest for the rapist's car. When he didn't find it right away he started to really worry. He was really that poor girl's only hope for escaping a hellish nightmare, and the thought of letting her down was unbearable for him. He knew he had to find that car, and he had to find it *fast*. There wouldn't be much time for searching—her time was running out.

There were few cars driving in the streets, and even fewer parked along the curbs, but he didn't see the one he was looking for. Even worse, he really had no idea which direction was the direction actually taken by the car, because the tiny dot on the screen had vanished at an intersection. The car could have continued on in any of three directions from that point without doubling back in his own direction where he would have spotted it. Though continuing straight ahead might seem the most probable route taken, no cars were seen up ahead traveling in that direction. It could just as easily have turned off to the left, or to the right at the intersection. There was no way at all to know where the car was headed.

The reality that he had lost the car and was completely unable to stop a violent crime from occurring, a violent crime that he knew was going to occur, was starting to sink in, and it was disturbing.

The tracking screen that faded out was another Luppert product. The single piece of equipment that might have saved an innocent person from harm in this case, and it failed him at the most critical moment. Until this, all of his products had served him well. But now there was nothing that could have been more frustrating for Trevor.

He steered his van toward the curb where it came to a fast stop. He left the engine running and grabbed up the device that was giving him so much grief, and took a closer look at it. He was disappointed with it enough to want to toss it out the window, but he knew that wouldn't solve the problem at hand.

A girl's life was at stake, and he felt the need to exhaust every possible option available, no matter how hopeless it seemed. The weight of the crisis was on his shoulders, and he felt it.

In seconds he had a screwdriver in his hands from the repair kit he always carried, and he quickly removed the floor plate on the device, exposing the circuit board. And in another instant his trained eye found the problem. A tiny circuit component had been shaken loose, and a critical part of the circuit was disconnected at that junction, interfering with the LED screen lights.

He wiped the sweat off his forehead with his left arm, and found a roll of adhesive tape in his repair kit with his right hand, tearing off an inch-long section and sticking it over the circuit component to hold it in place. With a short prayer he turned the unit on, and to his great relief the lights in the screen came back on.

Almost forty-five minutes later the car turned off from the highway it had been traveling on, onto a long weed-covered graveled drive, and followed it for almost a quarter of a mile toward an old dilapidated barn. There were no houses or any sign of inhabitants on the place. It was just an abandoned, secluded hideaway, with enough trees scattered around to keep nearly any activity private.

The car stopped close to the barn, and the man climbed out, dragging the crying girl by her hair out behind him, with his big knife still clutched tightly in the fist of his left hand.

She screamed, but not for long when she saw the futility in it. There was obviously nobody else around besides herself and the man within range of hearing, and she knew that her screams dissuaded his wickedness not at all.

The girl's sense that she would never see the light of day again after he forced her into the dark, dingy barn kept her struggling against his brutal persuasion, but his overpowering physical strength, augmented with the threat of the sharp blade, coerced her through the front door, which was close to falling off its hinges.

It seemed quiet inside, as someone might expect that early in the morning, with the exception of pigeons stirring in the rafters. The atmosphere was also pretty dim inside. The only light was the small amount of early daylight entering between the few broken wall boards, the loose front door, and the window openings above the loft. The sun was still rising, and the light rays cut through the inside darkness in almost horizontal beams, illuminating the dust particles that appeared to hang in the air. It smelled musty and dirty, like decaying hay mixed with bird droppings.

The man unzipped his pants with his right hand, and simultaneously yanked down smartly on the girl's uniform shirt collar with his left, tearing her shirt almost free from her frame. A second vigorous tug pulled it completely off of her, and with his right hand he excitedly unbuttoned her pants and jerked them down to her knees. His own pants had by then dropped down to his ankles. He had stabbed the knife into the wall where he alone would be able to easily reach it.

While he seemed suddenly preoccupied with getting himself undressed, she saw an opportunity to strike her fist into his groin, and convinced it might well be her only chance for escaping his control over her, she struck the hardest blow she could muster, and then tried to spring toward the door.

As he doubled over in pain, his left hand found one of her ankles and clamped onto it with a death grip, preventing her from getting away. Her interrupted motion sent her face down onto the dirt floor. She could hear him cursing and yelling angrily, and she tried to kick and struggle free but he wouldn't let go.

When she rolled onto her back and looked up, she saw him reaching for the big knife he'd stuck into the wallboards. He was in a rage. Again she tried to struggle free, but his grip was too strong. When he had the blade out of the wall, he raised it up over her for a dramatic stabbing, and it hit her like a charge of electrical current that this would be her end. She was frozen with fear in that split second period of time. She felt totally helpless to stop the angry maniac.

And then his head jerked back in the same instant she heard a loud gunshot. The big knife was flung across the barn by his reflex, and he sank back against a wall of hay, lifeless, his eyes frozen in a stare and a shocked look. Blood suddenly seemed to be splattered on everything around him, including her. When it occurred to her that she was finally free from his terror, she drew her leg in close to her, as if retaking possession of it.

The man silhouetted in the doorway of the barn was wearing a full ski mask to hide his identity, and he was holding a rifle.

"Who are you?" she asked as soon as she could utter words, "I don't understand. What's going on?"

Even in the dim light her frightened face was evident.

"I'm a vigilante. My aim is to stop people like him from harming people like you. I almost failed this time. I'm sorry I let him get this far."

She looked at the half-naked dead rapist, and shivered a little, "He would have killed me. How did you know we were here?"

"I've been following him. He's the serial rapist they let back out into society because of a technicality. Well, his raping days are over."

"What now?" she tried to cover her bare skin with a torn piece of her uniform.

"I've already called the police," he said, "I explained things. They should be up this road in about ten minutes. Give them your side of the story, everything just as it happened. You'll be all right."

"What are you going to do?"

"Leave before the police arrive, so that I can continue stopping people like him."

"I owe you for saving my life," she glanced back at the rapist, to make sure he was really no longer a threat, "I can't believe this all really happened. It's a nightmare. How will I ever…?"

When she looked back toward the door, he was already gone.

By the time Trevor's van reached the highway, he could already hear the sirens. He couldn't see the police cars, but they didn't sound far away. It had been a narrow escape for him, certainly too close for comfort, but in another moment his van was moving with the flow of traffic, as inconspicuously as every other vehicle on the road.

He started to feel a knot in his stomach. He had never taken the life of a human being before this day, and he wasn't liking the feeling he was getting about it. Even though he could rationalize the necessity of it, and he kept reminding himself that he had pulled the trigger to *save* a life, it still gave him an ugly feeling inside. He couldn't free himself from the notion that he had been acting in a capacity that he really had no right to. In a sense it was as if he'd been playing God with life and death, and he wasn't at all comfortable with it.

But despite the burden he was feeling, he well knew all along that it could come to that. All the time he was investing in expensive firearms and practicing his shooting skills, he understood that it might actually come down to him using them at some point. He was also aware of the simple fact that, had he not been so proficient and ready to employ weapons, that supermarket employee would have been raped and murdered. Ultimately he decided in his mind that the unpleasant task was worth the sacrifice.

Trevor knew the stakes were especially high for him now. A man who had been in the news a lot was now dead, shot in the back of the head while attempting to rape a new victim, and his case would no doubt be making headlines all over again—maybe the rapist would be even bigger news this time around. This was surely going to stir up the whole pot of reporters, police investigators, and everybody else looking for a story. Trevor realized he was going to have to really watch his step from now on, more than ever before. One tiny overlooked shred of evidence that might link him to the rapist's death could set the whole country to hunting him.

By now the wheels in his mind were turning at high speed. He started thinking about his surveillance devices in the dead man's apartment. An extremely thorough search could possibly find them, and there would be a lot of questions asked. He was careful enough to retrieve his tracking beacon from under the rapist's car before disappearing into the trees behind the barn, but his electronics in the apartment were still in place. He hadn't gotten the opportunity to retrieve them yet. He hadn't expected to be killing him. He wouldn't have pulled the trigger if the man didn't have that knife raised for stabbing. He'd have been able to prevent anyone from getting hurt, had he been there just a few seconds sooner. But he couldn't change things now. He did what he had to do, and that was that.

How long would it take investigators to begin combing the man's apartment? Probably not very long at all, he thought. The whole incident would surely be breaking news before the day was over, and a search warrant would no doubt be issued promptly. His only chance now was to beat the mad rush to the man's apartment and remove what he'd installed, and he took the most direct route to it. From the abandoned farm it was roughly an hour drive.

The morning was still early, before the big rush to work, and the traffic was light on the highway. Trevor was careful about the speed limits hoping to avoid unwanted attention, but he was anxious. When he got into the denser, more metropolitan part of Los Angeles, the traffic thickened. But it was still early enough that he was able to make reasonable time.

And then everything slowed way down. The traffic wasn't moving like it had been. And things continued slowing down until it was a snail crawl, bumper to bumper, and it soon came to a standstill.

Up ahead maybe half a mile where the road curved he could see the flashing lights. But it wouldn't very likely be roadwork, he told himself, because there hadn't been any such activity when he passed by coming from the opposite direction less than an hour before.

His van, right along with all the cars in front of him, was now stopped. For the time being at least nobody was moving. And there was no place anywhere nearby where anyone could turn off onto another road. He'd have to just sit there and be patient, because he didn't really have a choice.

He turned his engine off to save gas, not knowing how long the traffic delay was going to last, and he turned on his scanner to see if he could pick up any emergency communications. He heard bits and pieces, but wasn't able to piece together enough to determine the exact nature of the obstacle up ahead.

After a few minutes he was still sitting there not moving, and he started running out of patience. He started his engine again and turned on his little television set that was powered by the van's battery, and searched the channels for a station with local news. Six minutes later he caught the news report about the semi that had jack-knifed and flipped upside down, blocking the road until they had the equipment they needed at the scene to move it out of the way. They were working on the problem, they said, but their best estimate was that it would take another twenty minutes before they could direct the clogged up traffic around the obstacle.

Trevor wiped away the drops of perspiration forming on his forehead. He knew his window of opportunity was fast closing as he sat there unable to go anywhere. Had he taken a slower route, he might have arrived there by now.

Clearing the road took a bit longer than expected. It wasn't until forty minutes later that the long line of cars was finally directed past the huge wreck and Trevor could continue on his way. By the time he reached the street with the apartment, he saw that he was already too late. He watched two police cars parking in front, so he drove on without even slowing down.

CHAPTER IV

Like a good detective, Del had learned a good deal about Wendy. It was easy enough, because she was Trevor's sister, and the job he'd taken on necessitated learning a lot about him, and his history, which obviously included a lot about his sister.

But she still didn't know an awful lot about the man she'd hired. She really only knew that she was attracted to him, and that he was a thorough detective. He also seemed to be attracted to her as well. But she had almost no information about his personal life, and suddenly that seemed more important to her than everything else, besides finding her brother.

"Have you ever been married?" she finally asked him while they were reviewing all the known facts about Trevor's disappearance.

"No, but I almost was once. About nine years ago."

He paused, solemnly remembering another part of his life, "She eventually broke it off with me. She said it was because of the nature of my work."

"Law enforcement?"

"Exactly. She said she would be living a life with the constant worry that something bad would eventually happen to me, and that the stresses of my job would have a negative effect on our relationship, like driving me to drink."

"Did it?"

"No. I wasn't a heavy drinker before I joined the force, and I'm still not. Her worries were unfounded."

"Do you think you'll ever get married?" she asked, fishing for any inkling.

He was pretty sure he understood why she was inquiring, "It's possible. But it depends on a lot of different things."

"What are some of the things?"

"Well, obviously one of them is whether or not the woman I would choose would agree to marry me."

She felt encouraged by his words, but she was careful not to let it show.

"I doubt there would be any question about that," she remarked, almost regretting having brought up the subject, thinking she might have exposed her vulnerability.

No more than a minute after she spoke his phone rang, and he picked it up. It was his old work partner, Officer "Clay" Robins.

"Del, I'd be in a sling if anyone found out I was sharing evidence with someone outside the department, but you've inquired about this missing millionaire case, and I still owe you a favor. Just don't let this out."

"You know I won't, Clay. What do you have?"

"Well, you saw in the news where they found that serial rapist had been shot dead, supposedly by the guy who calls himself the Vigilante."

"I saw something about it, yeah. Didn't get all the details. What about it?"

"In our search of his apartment, we found an electronic listening bug and a tiny surveillance video camera."

"Not surprising, considering his pastime," commented Del.

"Right, but the reason it's significant is because he apparently never knew these things were in his apartment. They were well hidden, in order to spy on *him*, unless he put them there himself to create the appearance of being spied on. But we haven't yet figured out how that would make sense, especially now, after his death.

"And then, when we ran a trace on these devices we discovered they were all manufactured by Luppert Systems, the missing millionaire's company. We believe there's a connection."

Del was suddenly rather quiet. He certainly never expected to hear this kind of information.

Wendy didn't catch all of both sides of the conversation, but she heard enough to know it contained some relevant information, and she was anxious for Del to hang up so she could ask him about it.

"Del, you still there?" officer Robins finally asked, after about fifteen seconds of silence on the line. Wendy could see the look on his face—the wheels in his mind were turning.

"I'm still here. Thanks, Clay. I appreciate the call. Do you guys have any other leads?"

"Not right now, but as you well know we're working hard on it."

"Of course you are. Let me know if anything else turns up, okay?"

"We'll see. Don't forget how much trouble I'd be in if…"

"Don't worry so much, Clay. You know me," he paused again, "I sure didn't expect this information. It sure does add a twist to everything, that's the truth."

After hanging up, he turned to Wendy. She was looking at him with raised eyebrows, waiting for an explanation.

"I've got a question for you," he said, "and the answer to it could be a key piece in our puzzle."

"So, ask me," she impatiently urged.

"Is your brother capable of shooting and killing someone?"

She looked somewhat stunned by the question, "What did that Clay, or whatever his name is, tell you? Does he know anything about my brother? Is Trev in some kind of trouble?"

"That was Officer Robins from the Department. The two of us go back a long time. He says there is some evidence linking your brother to the shooting of that serial rapist the other day. From your point of view, could he have done that?"

She didn't provide a quick answer. She thought about it quietly, trying to imagine her brother shooting someone. It was difficult to imagine.

"He used to read plenty of gun books along with all of that spy literature he was always reading. I know that he owned some firearms—some rather exotic looking military-style rifles. I've seen them at his house a number of times. It was typical of Trev to collect things like that. And if you were to ask me whether or not he knew how to shoot, I'd say yes. He loved to shoot, just like he loved playing at martial arts and that sort of thing. But I just can't imagine him shooting at people. My brother isn't a killer. That just doesn't fit with his personality."

"Well, the police suspect he might be that vigilante we've been hearing about in the news. They're keeping a tight lid on it to keep their theory out of the media circus, but they've got some evidence to support it. Clay's always been a straight shooter since I've known him. I believe what he says. But if they're right, then you won't be needing me anymore to solve your mystery. They will have done it for you."

She shook her head, "No. I hired *you* to find my brother. They can come up with all the theories they want, and get all the evidence they'll ever need to support their theories, but I want to find my brother. I hope you'll stay on the job."

Delmar Mackenzie had a reputation among L.A. law enforcement for eagerly working the most difficult to solve cases, and he'd helped solve some of the toughest ones during his twenty-one years with the Department. But this case was really unique. After having worked on it for more than a week without turning up much to go on, he wasn't feeling particularly encouraged.

But the pay was good, even if he didn't feel like he was actually earning it. And Wendy was a worthy attraction. He felt himself drawn into her world, and he wasn't sure he had the strength, or even the slightest desire to resist. He'd never met anyone like her before. Perhaps he was falling in love, but he didn't want to think of it that way, whether true or not.

"I'll stay on for another week, if you wish, but after that if I don't have any leads, I think it would be pointless to continue."

She smiled, "A lot of things can happen in a week," she said.

Even as cleverly as he'd hidden his surveillance gear in the rapist's apartment, Trevor knew he should presume that the police would have uncovered at least some of it, and if so they'd be looking for him. Now, even more vital than before, would be his constant reliance on effective disguises. He would never again be free to relax or let his guard down. He'd chosen his path in life forever and sealed his fate with this unplanned situation. There could be no turning back.

At times he couldn't help wondering whether or not he'd lost his mind. Everything he'd given up to pursue his purpose was huge, even by his own standards. He'd made major sacrifices for this. But at the same time, he really understood that this was a course he had to take. This was a purpose for which he believed he'd been born, and just about everything in his life could be seen in some way or another as integral with his destiny.

And life was suddenly getting a lot more complicated. He had to exist and operate completely incognito all the time, which was certainly a challenge for someone of his status, but he would have to be especially careful in everything he did, and think of every small detail so as to avoid slipping up. It would be constant, and it would get old after awhile. But his life, and his mission, depended on his endurance with such things.

Living among society without leaving a paper trail was a challenge. Things like credit cards were generally impractical for him. He had his aliases, and Post Office boxes, but his best asset was the amount of cash he had stashed away hidden where only he had access to it. He carried several hundred thousand in fives, tens, and twenty-dollar bills within the upholstery of the van's seats. He'd buried another ten million in mixed bills under the ground, in a half dozen strategic locations where he could easily retrieve his caches without being seen. He used airtight stainless steel canisters to protect the money. He had a few hiding places for gold and silver coins as well, and in his own apartment (rented under one of his aliases) he kept a locked safe full of fifty and hundred-dollar bills, which added up to about sixty-four thousand dollars. He maintained a few bank accounts under various aliases, but was careful not to keep too much in any single account so as to avoid drawing attention. His biggest cache was his nearly forty million dollars in a Swiss bank, accessible only with an account number. He would make no financial transactions that could in any way be linked to Trevor Lupport.

He continued watching, listening, and spying. He also now tended to think of himself as a fugitive, operating under the reasonable presumption that he was a wanted man, even if a warrant for his arrest had yet to be announced in the media.

But his operations weren't going to be hindered by his worries about getting caught by the police. He knew he could elude them for a while. If anything, this situation would only make him want to try to be more careful, and definitely more alert than he might have otherwise been without the increased apprehension. And it encouraged him to suddenly work more aggressively at preventing crimes, knowing that his current freedom to operate would be coming to an end whenever they caught up with him. That, realistically thinking, would only be a matter of time now. So there was an awful lot to do in a potentially very short amount of time.

His "spy kit" resembled something out of an episode of *Mission Impossible.* He had a special shoulder bag full of pockets inside containing lock-picking tools, electrician's tools, binoculars, night vision optics, and various other high-tech gadgets one would expect to find in James Bond's kit. He had rubber gloves that closely resembled real skin, with near perfect skin coloring, ridges, hair and veins that were difficult to distinguish from the actual fingers, knuckles, and backs of a man's hands. Wearing them, Trevor could use his hands in a public environment without anyone knowing he was wearing gloves, while leaving behind no fingerprints by which to trace him. And he was making use of a wide variety of other nifty little products now, some of which he had designed himself and fabricated at Luppert Systems.

He had also become a master of disguises, and found himself changing his look sometimes twice a day, with a little extra attention to cosmetic detail while studying his face and figuring out how to change his features using an assortment of cosmetic products and the mirror inside his van. He'd grown more facial hair in recent weeks than he'd ever grown in his life, and he made himself quite difficult to recognize. He operated with such cognizance that, even if the general public knew the police were actively hunting him, and even if everyone knew that Trevor Luppert was the Vigilante, he wouldn't be easily identified.

The city of Los Angeles, with all of its sprawl, stretches in different directions for miles and is occupied by millions of people. That environment made it obviously impossible for an individual like Trevor, or even for an army of vigilantes like him to stop every crime. But the rumors and reports about his activity were certainly making a difference in the number of robberies, shootings, muggings, and rapes in the area. Some offenders quit their criminal activities altogether for the time being and waited anxiously for news of his capture. There was no way for anyone to know when and where he would appear to snare the next unsuspecting bad guy, because he was careful to avoid establishing any discernible patterns. He always seemed to come out of nowhere with perfect surprise and total control over the situation, snare his target, and then vanish before anyone could figure out where he had come from or where he had gone.

Pretty soon his activities were leading to the arrest of an average of one criminal per day. Occasionally he would hit the jackpot and deliver a whole gang of thieves or drug smugglers to the authorities, or prevent a really big crime from being committed. He knew his campaign against the crime world was having a real effect when he learned from his trusted informants on the streets that the top drug dealers and gangsters were offering cash for any information about him. It was a dangerous game he was playing, but it was exactly what he wanted. It was what he'd sacrificed greatly to achieve.

The pieces of the puzzle were fitting together perfectly now for Del. The theory that Trevor Luppert and the Vigilante were the same person certainly explained why Trevor would want the surveillance equipment from Luppert Systems that Walter

Collier had explained was missing from their inventory, along with their boss. It would also be consistent with Wendy's characterization of Trevor. It would take a purpose driven individual to devote himself to fighting crime full time like that. And on top of everything else, the Vigilante had to be somebody with considerable resources, and above-average intelligence. Everything seemed to fit Del's profile of Trevor.

The only problem was knowing where to look for him. Wendy wanted to find her brother, and talk to him. Convincing her that he was the Vigilante wasn't enough. She didn't seem to care a whole lot about that, anyway. The more she thought about it, the more she suspected it was probably true. But he was still her brother.

Finding him was promising to be a complicated task for Del. Not only had Trevor successfully eluded everyone else who'd been looking for him for months, which was a lot of different people, but now it was evident that he was well armed and had demonstrated his willingness to use deadly force in certain situations. Del carried his own sidearm, a customized 1911 .38 Super Automatic, but he only carried it for self-defense and never expected to have to use it. He was mindful that *if* he ever caught up with Trevor, he'd have to be especially careful.

The only way he would ever have a chance of finding him would be to learn to think like him, and envision himself in Trevor's position. Not an easy thing, considering how unusual Trevor's situation was. But Del taught himself to think like the people he searched for while he was a police detective, and the method worked as well or better than any other he had used.

Trevor was probably doing the same thing, Del guessed. He was probably imagining himself in the shoes of all those criminals, trying to stay a step ahead of them in their thought process. Whatever his technique, it was obviously working. But if it was likely that the Vigilante would be thinking like a criminal, then it was equally reasonable for anyone searching for the Vigilante to think like a criminal as well. That wouldn't be so easy for some of the people trying to find him. In a way, just about everything involving people involved certain thought processes, and psychology. Del understood the concepts. He'd attended plenty of seminars about psychological profiling used in law enforcement, and he'd studied the subject at length before employing many of the principles in his own detective work.

Following in the footsteps of a vigilante was a completely new experience for Del. He'd worked on cases involving some mighty strange people, but never a vigilante. He'd seen the movie, *Death Wish,* back in the seventies. There were certain parallels to the present scenario, but there were some major differences, too. This real-life vigilante was a lot more sophisticated than the fictional character. And Trevor Luppert, as near as Del had been given to understand, wasn't out for simple revenge. He was apparently obsessed with stopping crime for the betterment of society.

Unfortunately for someone like Trevor, and even for the whole of society in Del's view, the courts didn't always serve the same end. Were the police to catch him right now, he would very likely be tried for murder, even though his deadly actions clearly prevented a real murder from happening. The *real* murderer had been set free by the court system.

Del had been hired by Wendy to find Trevor, and that was what he was focused on right now. He no longer worked for the Los Angeles Police Department. If they wanted the Vigilante, they'd have to find him themselves. They certainly weren't going to be getting any help from Delmar Mackenzie.

He had gone over everything Wendy had having to do with her brother over and over again. He had by this time met with Walter Collier, and had talked with some of the other Luppert employees as well, some for the second or third time. He had interviewed everyone he could find who knew Trevor, and studied every letter, note, photograph, sketch, and scrap of potential physical evidence left behind by Trevor that he could get access to. He strained to glean any clue about where to find him from all of it, but kept coming up blank and frustrated.

Trevor left behind reams of sketches and blueprints he had created, some more refined than others. Many remained in locked storage in his office at Luppert Systems, where Mr. Collier preferred to keep them confidential to protect any technology they might contain, but many more were left in the huge apartment where Trevor had been residing. Those had already been available to the police, but none of it was considered by them to be useful.

Del was taking advantage of every opportunity he'd been given to view and study whatever documents he could find that were available to him with special permission. He took a look at literally hundreds of pages, hoping to discover even a single item that might somehow help his search.

The only thing he found that managed to catch his attention was a simple sketch of a full-sized van, heavily covered with handwritten notes outlining a number of custom modifications. It looked like he had drawn it at his kitchen table while eating breakfast or while watching T.V., because it was obviously a free-handed quickie sketch. It caught Del's attention because it didn't seem to fit in with the rest of the material he'd come across. It looked like more of a casual drafting of some very general ideas. And the van in the drawing—he wondered what it might be needed for. The notes indicated ballistic armor lining in the vehicle's body, and a periscope in the roof. Were security vehicles on the drawing board at Luppert Systems?

When Del questioned Walter Collier about this, he insisted they had no plans for producing any automobile components. Walter had no knowledge of any van such as depicted in Trevor's drawing.

"He didn't own a vehicle like that that I was aware of," Walter explained, "He'd mentioned a couple times that he was considering buying a new Hummer, but I never heard anything about a van. As far as I know, he never even bought a Hummer. Trevor liked things like 4x4 pickups quite a lot, more than sports cars. Of course, he could afford any kind of rig he wanted."

"If he was to have such a vehicle custom built, who would he go to, to build it for him?" Del asked, while Walter stared at Trevor's sketch.

"I don't know anybody in Los Angeles who builds security vehicles, but I've heard of a company in Mexico that specializes in that sort of thing. There's apparently a strong demand for them down there, because they have so many dangerous areas these days," he said, smiling. "This is funny, because Trevor took a two-week trip to Mexico last year. I have to admit I never really understood what the attraction was with Mexico. He could have gone to Europe, or the Far East. Anywhere he wanted to go, but he went to Mexico."

"I'll see what I can find out on the internet about these security vehicle specialists," said Del, "It might not turn up anything, but my job is to follow up every possible lead. I appreciate all your trouble, Mr. Collier."

"No trouble at all. We're as anxious to see him return as everyone else is. You don't suppose he's taking an extended vacation down in Mexico somewhere, do you?"

Del shook his head, "No, I don't. I try not to rule anything out, but I'm pretty sure he's not in Mexico."

Trevor hadn't seen his baby sister in almost three months. He knew the rule about contacting family or friends. That's how most fugitives usually end up blowing their cover. Instructional books on hiding out always advise against it. It would simply be too risky to call her or show up at her door. Even as much as he trusted her, the authorities or some reporter could be expected to be watching her, waiting for just such a contact. As much as he wanted to, it would simply be too risky, and he knew it.

He might get away with sending her a card in the mail, but it was still too early even for that. He decided it was better all the way around if she didn't know anything about his situation, whether he was alive or dead, or where he lived. What she didn't know couldn't be used against him, he told himself. He needed to keep things as simple as possible.

But he needed to know that she was getting along okay. He needed to check on her, even if he wasn't ready to establish any communication.

He drove by her apartment early, before she normally left for her morning run. He saw that her car was in its regular space, but he noticed that there was a car in the guest parking space as well. It wasn't a car he'd ever seen there before. In fact, he couldn't remember when he'd ever seen any car in either of her two parking spaces besides hers.

This sparked his curiosity. Maybe she had a friend staying over. The car had a California license plate, so whoever it was didn't have to travel from out of state to see her. Finding that car there at that early hour meant its owner had most likely spent the night.

Even though he understood this was really her business, he couldn't leave it alone. His mind shuffled through a series of possibilities, including the unlikely scenario that the car was the vehicle of some undercover agent of law enforcement involved in some kind of round-the-clock surveillance scheme using Wendy as a decoy to lure him in. Perhaps that was an unreasonable suspicion, but in his position, Trevor felt he had to consider everything.

The only way to find out who belonged to that car would be to plant himself somewhere within view and watch to see who besides Wendy came out of her apartment. It might even be worthwhile attaching a tracking beacon to the car, if he could do it without being spotted. His window of opportunity for that would be short, because it wouldn't be long before she would appear outside for her regular morning jogging routine.

The little transmitter was easy and quick to attach to the underside of a car because it was mounted to a strong magnetic platform. Presuming it had a fresh battery, employing it required only turning on the switch, extending the antenna, and sticking its base to a spot under the car where it wouldn't be seen.

Six o'clock in the morning was before most people were leaving for work. And there weren't any barking dogs near the apartment complex, so Trevor, after parking his van around the block, was able to discreetly creep up to the car on foot, plant the device and then disappear without being noticed. He wore soft silent moccasins whenever he needed to walk with stealth. He had learned how to move without making a sound.

Leaving his van parked out of view, he grabbed a pair of 10x binoculars and melted into a row of hedges across the street some two hundred yards from Wendy's apartment, where he had a clear view of her door.

Like clockwork she exited her apartment wearing her jogging suit at precisely 6:30. But she wasn't alone this morning. A man stepped out of the apartment right behind her, also wearing typical running clothes. The two of them walked together down the walkway toward the end of the driveway where they started jogging on the far side of the street.

Trevor centered the man's face in his binoculars, trying to determine if he was anyone he knew. He didn't look familiar. Soon Wendy and the man were around the block out of view.

Suddenly the identity of this guy, who was apparently spending time with his sister, seemed important. Trevor would find out who he was. He would track his car when he left and learn more about him.

Less than two hours later he followed the man's car through the heavy morning traffic, not more than a few miles, and subsequently watched him unlock the door of an office to open for business. The sign painted on the front window said *Delmar Mackenzie's Professional Investigative Services.* That name, Delmar Mackenzie, rang familiar in his head, but he wasn't sure why. Anyway, this man was a private investigator, and he'd spent the night with Wendy. Trevor *had* to find out more about him.

CHAPTER V

Speculation about the Vigilante seemed to spread like a flu virus across Los Angeles, as the arrests of criminals resulting from his activities continued to grow in number.

Leo Malone ran the West Coast segment of the Malone family business, which had its fingers, in one way or another, in a dozen states across the country. He still spoke in his New York/Italian accent, but he'd set up his slice of the organization in Los Angeles decades ago. He preferred the warmer weather, and besides, he never got along very well with his three brothers or with either of his two first cousins. They all thought of him as a dangerous loose cannon with a bad temper who was generally careless in his business dealings.

There existed a secret agreement among the other members of the family that if Leo ever managed to get himself arrested, his life was to be quickly shortened "accidentally" before he had a chance to spill any beans on the rest of them. They considered him high risk. He never knew about their little agreement, but he never trusted any of them anyway. His nearest brother ran a casino in Las Vegas, and that was as close as he cared to be with any of them.

Now his mind was consumed with hunting the Vigilante, and most of his time and resources were being devoted to that end. As much as he deplored any perception that he might be intimidated at all by an individual he couldn't even identify, the reality was that all of his profitable business activities were very much threatened by this man. The situation had to be dealt with and this problem resolved swiftly. He had all of his people working on it, and he was fast running out of patience.

The breakthrough in the manhunt finally came when one of Trevor's street sources for information decided to sell his knowledge about the Vigilante to Leo Malone for an irresistible sum of cash. It was the scenario Trevor worried about most, because he used a number of street sources, most of whom would sell out their own mothers for the right price. He guessed it would only be a matter of time until this happened. And he wouldn't likely know about it until it was too late, as he had no effective way currently to closely monitor Malone or his men. They'd discovered all the bugs he had planted, and it was too risky now to plant new ones. The best he could do now was to intercept some of their radio and telephone conversations, but that probably wouldn't yield much. They would be careful in how they used conventional systems of communication.

Because Trevor used disguises and aliases, his true identity wasn't available for sale on the street. But the source knew when and where the Vigilante could be contacted to deliver information, and that by itself was worth whatever the cost to Malone. The crime boss didn't mind paying the rogue opportunist because, after he had the information he wanted, it would be a simple matter reclaiming the money before dumping the man's corpse into the sewer.

The authorities had known about Leo Malone's drug dealings for quite some time, as his reputation made him notorious. But even as careless as he often was in some ways, he had remained remarkably lucky thus far. The police had yet been unable to assemble sufficient evidence to make an arrest. Mainly, they hadn't been able to convince any of the "small fish" they'd arrested to testify against him. There was the general belief that doing so would be suicidal. Malone miraculously managed to stay one step ahead of them.

Del knew quite a bit about Leo Malone. He knew all about his reputation, and how he ruled the streets with his brutal methods of intimidation. He also suspected that such a key piece on the chessboard would be a likely target for Trevor's war against crime, given his reputation, and L.A.P.D.'s inability to put him behind bars. When Del heard through the grapevine that Malone lost over three-quarters of a million dollars to someone he couldn't identify, he couldn't avoid the urge to smile. He had a mental picture of Malone's angry face.

It seemed reasonable to believe that if Malone was being plagued by the Vigilante, then watching him ought to be the surest way to find Trevor Luppert, if all other suspicions about the Vigilante were accurate. And Del had possibly one piece of the puzzle already, which nobody else looking for Trevor would be likely to have, and that was the knowledge, as limited as it was, about the van.

There were obviously plenty of other vans on the road, and it seemed logical that Trevor would have gone out of his way to have his van built as inconspicuous as possible. It was even conceivable that Trevor's illustration remained only an idea in his head, and that an operational vehicle never actually materialized from it. But Del had been studying Trevor's ways of thinking, and he felt confident the van did in fact exist, and that it was as amazingly sophisticated as could be imagined. It would be perfectly consistent with Trevor's way of doing things.

With a bit of research, Del found a shop in Mexico City that specialized in customizing security vehicles and offering a wide range of specialty features, such as bullet-proofing the vehicle body and installing a variety of high-tech gadgets. It was a likely shop to build Trevor's van. But just as Del expected, their customers' names were kept confidential.

He understood that the only way anyone would have any reasonable chance of finding Trevor would be to follow in his footsteps. He would have to talk to the same people Trevor talked to, watch the same people Trevor watched, and try to focus on all the same concerns Trevor obviously had to focus on.

Del knew a few people he could rely on for information, too, from his days as a street cop. A cop makes his share of enemies, but if he's anything above a hard-nosed jerk, he makes a few friends around town as well. And those friends can be mighty useful when one needs them. People see things, and people hear things. A little information can be invaluable when working on a difficult case. Del had discovered that a long time ago.

The Vigilante hadn't confined himself to any particular segment of Los Angeles. The police weren't able to decipher any patterns to his operations. And since they couldn't pin down any specific part of the city he might prefer over another, they weren't able to concentrate their search.

Del was a fine detective, but the only plan he had at the moment was to keep a close watch on Leo Malone. If the crime boss was being harassed by the Vigilante, then maybe his daily routines were worth following. Something interesting might turn up. It was just a hunch, but it was the only idea he currently had. The rumors on the streets suggested it might be worth a shot, although he also wondered if it wasn't just a waste of time.

Del had done his homework a while ago on Leo Malone, during a police investigation. He knew where he lived, and where he maintained his office. He even knew the names and faces of some of his accomplices. The L.A. Police had squandered plenty of their resources watching him, until they eventually decided that their efforts might be more productive some other way.

Del went to Walter Collier for advice on surveillance equipment, and was rewarded with the loan of some very sophisticated gear. There was an eagerness among everyone at Luppert to help Del, because they all wanted Trevor found, and the fact that Del was now a private investigator working for Trevor's sister made his position a trusted one. Regardless of whatever Trevor might be up to, none of his employees wanted to see him scooped up by the police, or the publicity that would likely follow. They all had their fill of the unrelenting publicity and that kind of atmosphere for a while after his disappearance. They simply wanted everything to return to the way things had been before all of it, if that was at all possible.

Walter was explaining the operational features of some of their most popular products, trying to determine which devices might be the most beneficial to Del's investigation. While Del was listening to him, he noticed several detailed blueprints on Walter's desk, and after Walter finished, Del pointed at them.

"Looks like your work is cut out for you," he said.

Walter glanced down at his desktop, "Oh yeah, this was an interesting concept. We've been calling it a sound restoring thermal imaging device, for lack of a better description. We're still trying to perfect it. We've done a prototype from Trevor's blueprint, but it needs further refining before we can sell it to government agencies, etc. We haven't had the opportunity to field test it yet."

"What exactly does it do?" Del sounded intrigued.

"It's supposed to see people through walls and hear what they say to each other. Our prototype picks up thermal shapes, but they aren't clear enough to determine who's who. That limits its usefulness. It was designed primarily for hostage rescue, but it needs more refining. We really need Trevor for that. He's the expert on thermal imaging."

"Does it pick up conversations through walls?"

"That part of it seems to be working pretty well, with careful tuning. It's a bit temperamental. The operator has to work with it for a while before it will function reliably. Sort of like an old transistor radio. It requires constant tuning."

"Why wouldn't Trevor have taken that prototype with him, along with all that other gear he left with?" Del asked, "Seems like a handy device, even if it could be refined more."

"I'm sure he would have, if we had it then. This device is new. We started assembling it, using his design, *after* he disappeared."

"Well, I'd sure be happy to field test it for you, if I might be permitted."

Walter was quiet for an instant. He looked at Del, considering his request.

"Yes, I think that's an excellent idea, Mr. Mackenzie," he stood up out of his chair, "If you'd be ready for a demonstration, we'll show you how this thing works."

Del knew where Leo Malone lived, but it wasn't an easy home to spy on by any means, with its elaborate security systems, electric outer fence, and ring of trees blocking any street view to the property. There were also security guards and guard dogs on the premises around the clock, making any sort of covert intrusion out of the question for Del. The limited information he had about the property came from the occasional police helicopter flights over the Beverly Hills neighborhood during the last year and a half or so. Del realized it wouldn't be practical to attempt to monitor Malone in his home.

Malone's office was a completely different situation. He maintained his office in a high-rise in the city where Del was able to aim the Luppert sound restoring device at the large grand view window from across the street, and listen to him talk. Ironically, Malone spent more time in his plush office than in his secluded home. Perhaps he felt he could work more effectively from his office.

Del was able to operate the device from his car, relatively inconspicuously he discovered, by lying down in the back seat where he wouldn't easily be seen, and with his window rolled down, aiming the device in the direction of Malone's seventh floor window. He was amazed at how clearly he could hear the voices conversing within the office, once he had it tuned in properly.

The device had a built-in recording system, to capture what could be heard for further analysis later. When Del heard the word "Vigilante", he pushed the record button and kept the device steady, and periodically adjusted the tuning knob to keep the reception as clear as possible.

This was almost as good as a listening device inside the room, except that it took constant attention to keep it tuned and aimed in the right direction. If the operator panned across the building's outer wall, different voices and conversations would fade in and out as if spinning the dial on an AM radio. But it was obviously a lot safer to operate this device than to attempt breaking into the office to plant a bug.

Del was impressed with Trevor's invention, and felt privileged to use it, especially since its inventor had not yet had the opportunity to do so. After a little practice, he became comfortably proficient with it, capturing certain important conversations he would never have heard otherwise.

And he was startled to hear what he heard. Malone's voice couldn't be mistaken with anyone else's, and the manner in which he spoke made it clear to any listener that he was the chief in the room. He seemed to command more than communicate. But when Del suddenly heard someone else in the room explaining when and where they could expect to find the Vigilante, he wasn't the only one who quietly and attentively listened. This was amazing information. And he'd gotten it on tape, which was even more amazing.

The images on the screen were more like indistinct orange shapes than actual human silhouettes, with a serious lack of detail to their form. But as vague as the picture was, there was still a three dimensional aspect to it, and Del was able to speculate with reasonable certainty that the figure apparently sitting behind his desk was Leo Malone. And when Malone eventually stood up from his chair and walked toward the huge window, Del could feel a chill run through his veins.

He held his breath and listened intently to every word Malone spoke, straining to determine whether the powerful crime lord would notice him down there on the street, monitoring the whole conversation from the back seat of his car. Del heard some words, but couldn't make them out. They weren't loud enough or clear enough. And he couldn't tell who in the office was speaking. He strained harder to listen, but still couldn't make sense of some of the words, and this was a critical moment. He could only lie there motionless with the device and *hope* that Malone wouldn't see him.

And then suddenly the human silhouette moved away from the window and back toward the office interior, finally sitting down apparently behind his desk, which wasn't visible on the screen. The conversation became more discernible when orders were dictated, but Del didn't need to hear more. He presumed he hadn't been noticed.

He'd heard, and recorded, the information he was hoping for but certainly had not expected. It was really almost too good to be true. But he felt that now was a good time to climb back into the driver's seat of his car and drive away, before his efforts were compromised. He didn't have a chance to write down the details of what he'd heard, but he'd gotten it on tape, and that was good enough. He could analyze it later for the important information.

Del heard enough to know what Malone planned to do, and when and where he planned to do it. There was a contact place and time when the Vigilante was expected to show up for an information update. It was under a bridge. Del was able to find the bridge on his map. He could scout around the place ahead of time and figure out the best position, if he could find one, from which to monitor everything without being noticed.

This was a risky situation. Malone obviously wanted to kill the Vigilante, but presumably only after interrogating him for all the information he possessed. No doubt Malone was a man with a hot temper, but he was no fool. If the Vigilante kept any incriminating evidence on Malone's activities, he'd want to get his hands on it before anyone else did. If he killed him right away, he could be destroying his best opportunity for gathering any information. He would know better.

Almost an hour later Del was certain he had found the bridge described in Malone's office, and he parked his car a few hundred yards away before taking his casual walk to explore the area.

He carried his Colt .38 Super Auto pistol in a shoulder holster under his jacket in case he ran into trouble. The expected meeting between the man who had sold out to Malone and the Vigilante wasn't for three more days, but this was a rough part of town. The sides of the bridge were decorated with gang graffiti, and it was a trashy place. Currently the area was pretty quiet.

He tried to imagine where the meeting might take place exactly, and where he might be able to monitor the location from a position where he wouldn't likely be seen. There were a few patches of small trees on both sides of the railroad tracks that passed under the bridge, and there appeared to be plenty of places to hide. There was also a lot of tall grass. It wouldn't be too hard to pick a spot with a good view straight under the bridge, especially if he crawled into position two hours or more before the time of the meeting.

As he made his way back up the hill to the road he heard the unmistakable sound of someone whispering coming from the bushes not far up ahead along the foot trail. He tried to ignore it and continue walking. As he approached the vicinity from which he knew he'd heard someone, the bushes rustled and a figure stepped out into the open in front of him, obviously intending to block his path.

It was a juvenile male, presumably a member of some gang as symbolized by his clothing. Then a second gang member stepped out of the bushes right behind the first. In another instant each had a switchblade knife in his hand with the blade open. The look on their faces was a look of aggression.

"Shouldn't you boys be in school right now?" Del asked them.

"Who you callin' 'boys'?" snapped the first one, holding his knife up in front of him.

Del looked at the knife, then into the juvenile's eyes, "Even if you stabbed me with that little thing, it would probably take a couple hours for me to bleed enough to loose my strength."

He slowly reached under his jacket and removed his pistol from its holster, flipping the safety down with his thumb in the process and aimed it at the closest one with a knife, "I ought to be able to do a lot of target shooting in that amount of time, don't you think? I use hollow points, and they make an awful mess. Kind of a shame to rip such huge holes in those fine clothes you're wearing. But we can play that game if you want."

Suddenly the closest juvenile closed his knife and dropped it into his pocket, then raised his open hands in the air to show he held no weapon, and started slowly backing away. The second followed his example, and the two of them soon disappeared into the bushes.

Del kept his gun in his hand, but flipped the safety back on, and with the same arm wiped away the tiny beads of sweat that had started forming on his forehead. He returned to his car as quickly as he could and walked all the way around it twice, inspecting it for signs of tampering. It appeared not to have been messed with, and he made a sigh of relief.

Trevor sure chose an awful part of the city to conduct his business affairs in, Del was thinking as he drove away. And his mind was swarming with questions about the predicted meeting in three days. He wondered how the "Vigilante" was going to come dressed for the occasion, and how he might possibly recognize him. He'd seen plenty of pictures of Trevor, but it was almost certain that he would have significantly altered his appearance, considering how well known Trevor Luppert's face was.

Del had a time and place now where the Vigilante was expected to show up all right, but there were plenty of unknowns still. And planning a surveillance operation was a complicated matter. It would be like trying to beat a master at his own game, and in this case the master was something of a genius.

And to make everything even more interesting, the Mafia was apparently setting a trap for the Vigilante, and it was promising to be a dangerously risky adventure by anybody's standards. There was an awful lot for Del to consider here.

As much as Del did *not* want to involve Wendy in this, he knew he couldn't avoid it. For one thing, a reliable surveillance operation around the bridge could certainly be accomplished much easier with two sets of eyes and ears than just one. And more important than that, he had to keep reminding himself that he was working for her, and she expected to be kept informed about events and any new leads that developed. And anyway, he was going to need her help with this, even if it was going to be dangerous.

By the time he got around to talking to her, he already had a basic plan sketched out. It would involve stationing her up on the road where she could watch motor vehicles traveling into or out of the area. Meanwhile he would be positioned on the hillside below the road where he would have a clear view under the bridge, where the meeting was supposed to take place. They would be able to communicate via 49 MHz voice-activated radio headsets, which had a range of about 400 yards.

She could be watching the road from his parked car or near it, and her location would theoretically be a safer one than his because of the exposure to regular automobile traffic. Most of the evidence of gang activity seemed to be present closely around and under the bridge, which was a location mostly hidden from regular public view.

But she and Del would maintain constant radio communication, so he would know immediately if she came into any danger. She would also be armed with a large can of full-strength pepper spray, just in case she needed a means of self-defense before he could reach her. But she didn't appear to be at all afraid as he outlined his plans. They went over the map he'd sketched of the area around the bridge, to help her become oriented with everything according to his strategy.

"If at some point you believe you've spotted Trevor," said Del, "it's critical that we stick close to the original program. Just let me know what you see. It's absolutely critical that we don't blow our cover, for his safety as well as for ours. That bridge is definitely not the best place for family reunions. If we do this thing right, you'll get your opportunity to see your brother very soon, in a safer environment where we won't have to deal with Malone's people, or a bunch of drug-peddling gang members."

She didn't argue. "I understand," she said.

What they weren't aware of was that Trevor had been watching them since he'd learned who Delmar Mackenzie was, and he'd gotten into each of their apartments, and into each of their cars to plant microphones, and he had also attached tracking beacons under their cars. He was certain their search for him was with the best intentions, at least he could say that about Wendy, and the private investigator was obviously working for her. But he wasn't ready to be found just yet, so he continued to monitor them.

Now he had learned by eavesdropping on his sister and her investigator that Malone had a trap waiting for him to walk into. This information was invaluable. And he also learned to his surprise that his theories on listening behind walls were being put to the test, and his schematic for a thermal viewing/listening device was a pretty good one. He didn't have easy access now to the sort of shop and tooling needed to fabricate such a unit, but he could still lay it out on paper. He still had the financial resources to build whatever he wanted, but not without involving others and likely drawing attention to himself. This investigator, Mackenzie, had the advantage of being able to field test his design. Trevor listened with pride as Del described the product to his own sister. The device would surely attract another juicy government contract for Luppert Systems, but Trevor felt he had more important issues to concern himself with now.

After listening to Del and Wendy for several days, Trevor learned more than he would ever have expected. Now he knew for certain that the police were looking for him in connection with the shooting of that rapist. He no longer had to wonder about that. And he learned exactly how Malone planned to set his trap. Del and Wendy replayed the recording of Malone's office meeting several times, and Trevor listened closely. A lot of important details were captured on that recording.

Wendy was now convinced that Trevor was indeed the Vigilante, and now Trevor knew she knew it. Fortunately, he thought, she wasn't running to the police with what she knew, though she probably didn't have much they could use, anyway. And this investigator, Mackenzie, was no longer working for the police. Trevor closely monitored him long enough to be completely satisfied that he wasn't reporting his information to the police.

But just what he should do with all of this new information presented something of a dilemma. If he showed up at the bridge as he was expected, he was walking into a trap. He couldn't ignore the risk factor in that. And if he didn't show up, Malone would likely get suspicious, and a lot more careful.

The worst part about all of this was knowing that Wendy and Mackenzie were going to be at the bridge, looking for him, and that would be a dangerous place for them to be looking for him. He was mindful that it was *his* actions that led to their plans.

He continued eavesdropping until he had all the details of their plan. Wendy was to be in Mackenzie's car, parked on the side of the road a few hundred yards from the bridge, where she had the best view of the road in both directions. She would use his best binoculars in her surveillance. Mackenzie planned to hide himself closer to the bridge and wait for the meeting to take place. It became evident to Trevor that Mackenzie's primary job, according to the plan, would be to prevent Malone's people from taking the Vigilante hostage. Basically, Trevor learned, this private investigator would be putting himself into a dangerous situation to protect him. He obviously considered it as simply doing his job—fulfilling his professional obligation. That may have seemed foolish from a practical view of everything, but Trevor understood it. It was precisely the sort of thing he could see himself doing.

Trevor listened from his van parked around the block behind his sister's apartment, as she and her investigator went over the details of their plan. He'd learned what Malone planned to do, and what Wendy and Mackenzie planned to do. Now it was time for him to figure out exactly what *he* should do. This kind of risky business warranted considerable thought. Whatever plan he came up with would have to be good. It would have to be very, very good, and there would be no allowance for even a single mistake. He would have to plan his strategy with patient attention to every detail. He understood the scope of the danger involved with it.

CHAPTER VI

The meeting location under the bridge was originally chosen by the man Trevor knew only as Sticky. Trevor never found out the real reason the man went by that nickname. He guessed it had something to do with his talent for lifting wallets, as he appeared to be living pretty well in the streets without any kind of regular job, and he never saw the man begging like so many others. It just seemed to explain it. He sure didn't look like a pimp or a drug dealer. Trevor was introduced to him by another street information source, and he had a bit of an uneasy feeling about him from the start, but the information Sticky sold him generally turned out to be accurate.

They would meet at the bridge once a week on a different day and at a different time each week, and Trevor would pay him a hundred dollars for any possibly useful information he had to share. If he thought the information was especially worthy, he'd give Sticky an extra hundred-dollar bill. But he was careful to keep his wallet secured in a zipped pouch inside his shirt where he could feel it against his stomach. And Sticky knew the Vigilante carried a gun.

He wasn't surprised that Sticky sold him out to Malone. He never trusted him, anyway. The only surprising thing about it was that Sticky would want to deal with Malone. That would take a lot of nerve, given Malone's reputation. Maybe the danger was somehow part of the attraction. Maybe. But more likely it was pure greed. He must have been pretty confident that he could demand a king's ransom from Malone. He must have been banking on Malone's burning need to rid his streets of the Vigilante. But the whole idea seemed crazy to Trevor. Malone was a wicked and dangerous man. How did Sticky expect to collect his payment and then walk away?

As hard as he tried, Trevor was never able to completely understand that back stabbing nature so common among criminals. But he knew enough about Leo Malone to know that when he no longer had use for people, he usually had them killed. Sticky was probably no exception.

After giving it a lot of thought, he finally decided to show up under the bridge at the previously agreed time. It was something he'd started, and he felt he had to see it through to whatever end would come of it.

He parked his van on a totally different road, outside of Wendy's view, and walked to the bridge from a quarter of a mile away, following the railroad track to the meeting place. This time he came armed with a pistol; a Browning Hi-Power 9mm in a hidden holster riding in the small of his back. He had every reason to expect trouble.

He knew he was being watched. Delmar Mackenzie would be watching through binoculars from the hillside bushes on one side of the tracks or the other, ready to interfere when the trouble started. Malone's people were probably also hidden in nearby bushes, waiting to spring their trap.

There was no certainty about whether or not Sticky would show. If he were going to, it would be pretty soon. If Malone were playing it smart, he'd use Sticky in this part of his plan, waiting until *after* he had the Vigilante before getting rid of him.

Pretty soon he saw somebody walking along the tracks, coming toward the bridge from the opposite direction. At first the person was too far away to identify. It wasn't uncommon to see people wandering up and down the tracks, and there was plenty of gang graffiti painted on the sides of the bridge. It could also have been one of Malone's people, or really anybody else.

Trevor recognized the walk when the person was about four hundred yards away. It was Sticky, all right. Trevor glanced at his watch and noticed that the meeting time was only two and a half minutes away.

"That's the one thing I like about you, Sticky," he said, almost whispering while Sticky was still too far away to hear him even if he shouted, "Always on time. But that's the *only* thing I like about you."

When he was within speaking distance, Trevor didn't say anything. He just waited and observed. Sticky's eyes scanned the surroundings, as if worried about something, and then he looked at Trevor.

"Got a surprise for you today," he said.

"I'm all ears," Trevor said, reaching into his zippered pouch and removing his wallet, "Today I came prepared to properly reward you. Your last tip was especially useful."

Sticky reached under his own windbreaker and nervously pulled out a pistol, pointing it at Trevor.

"Unfortunately, I'm not talkin' about the kind of surprise you're prob'ly hopin' for. I know you carry a gun, so...Let's have it out where we can see it, nice and slow. And I'll have that wallet, too, thanks," he yanked the wallet out of Trevor's hand.

Trevor proceeded to slowly remove his gun from its holster, and held it up where Sticky could see it wasn't in a firing position.

"Now toss it into the bushes," Sticky ordered.

Trevor complied, flinging the pistol off to the side. As he did he watched where it went from the corner of his eye, and heard it land in the weeds. He tried to make a mental note of the location.

"How much is Malone paying you?" Trevor asked.

"A hell of a lot of money, that's all I'm gonna say."

"Have you seen any of it yet?"

"Ten percent. I'll get the balance when I deliver you to his people. So let's get going. You're going to walk in front of me so I can keep an eye on you. And don't try any tricks."

Trevor did as Sticky ordered, slowly walking ahead of him, wondering what ever happened to that detective, Mackenzie. He looked around, but saw no sign of anyone. He started sorting through a series of scenarios in his head, searching for ideas.

"Do you honestly believe that Malone will let you live after he gets what he wants? Think about it. You know too much. And he knows you'd sell him out, just like you sold me out. What do you figure the chances are you'll ever see that other ninety percent? I'm really surprised at you, Sticky. Knew you were greedy and figured you weren't entirely trustworthy, but I never took you for a sucker."

"Shut up!" Sticky yelled nervously, then quickly looked around to make sure nobody else was around, "Just keep walkin', and keep quiet. Don't want to be forced to fill you with holes and take all the fun away from the man who's payin' me proper."

Trevor guessed that Sticky would probably pull the trigger if he were startled. He may have been a pickpocket, but he obviously wasn't experienced in armed robbery. He was nervous. Trevor could see that if he were to make a move, he would have to be lightning fast, and he'd have to be sure it was the right opportunity. But if he waited too long, it could be too late. Once he'd been handed over to Malone's people, the situation would be a lot more complicated.

After they had walked several hundred yards, Trevor stopped and turned around. Sticky gripped his pistol with both hands, appearing suspicious if not downright annoyed at the interruption in movement.

"What are you doing?" he demanded.

"Look, Sticky, what if I doubled Malone's offer? Would that be worth it to you, and get you playing this game my way?"

Sticky appeared to consider. Then his eyes narrowed.

"I know a trick when I smell one," he said, "Besides, I'd have Malone gunnin' for me for sure if I did that. I'd have to be a real fool to try something so suicidal. You better turn back around and keep walkin.'"

Trevor assessed his position and contemplated throwing a roundhouse kick to disable Sticky's right arm, as he was a right-handed shooter. He believed he could do it swift enough for a successful result, *probably*. But it would certainly be risky. And there wasn't a lot of time to be thinking about it. Sticky was getting more anxious the longer they stood there. He might even accidentally pull the trigger.

Trevor was rehearsing his move in his mind when something caught his attention, distracting him. A branch moved in the shrubs on the hillside across the tracks, maybe forty yards away. Sticky instinctively turned his head in the direction Trevor was looking, but saw nothing. He turned back around quickly when he realized he'd taken his attention off the Vigilante. Trevor didn't see who or what caused the branch to move, but he quickly realized he'd missed a perfect opportunity to catch Sticky off guard. Suddenly Sticky became more suspicious. He wouldn't likely take his eyes off Trevor again anytime soon, now expecting a trick.

Trevor turned back around and continued walking, and thinking. He wasn't too worried. He was sure he would get another chance to take control of the situation one way or another. Besides, he was a little bit curious to find out how everything would happen, and how many men Malone would send to collect him.

He kept hearing noises in the bushes on the one hillside, but he didn't turn back to look. It sounded like somebody was probably following and watching them. But it could just as easily have been a stray dog or coyote. Whatever it was didn't make a huge amount of noise. Sticky didn't seem to notice.

The gorge gradually bent around a low knoll, and the terrain opened up where the tracks paralleled a residential street for about five hundred yards. The edge of the field nearest the street was lined with a wall of tall eucalyptus trees, presumably as a noise barrier for when the train tooted its horn coming around the bend.

Trevor noticed a late model Lincoln parked on the street, just behind those trees. Sticky began directing him toward the car, and he knew it had to be occupied by Malone's people.

As they approached the car, one of the doors opened and a man stepped out, holding the door open for the Vigilante. Trevor realized that if he got into that car, his chances for gaining any kind of upper hand would be severely limited. And it was difficult for him to determine exactly how many of them there were in that car—maybe three or four. But he didn't see a very good opportunity for resisting at the moment, with Sticky's gun pointed at his back. He started feeling like he'd crawled between a rock and hard place.

And then everything changed with the sound of a gunshot. The distraction was enough to prompt Trevor into action, and act he did, swiftly and decisively with the heel of his shoe catching Sticky's right elbow with enough force to break his arm and send his pistol ten feet into the air.

A second gunshot persuaded the man who'd been holding the car door open back into the car, quickly closing the door after him. It was impossible for Trevor to determine immediately what the shooting was all about, or just who was shooting at whom, but he didn't waste time trying to figure it out. It was a distraction, and that was all that he could have hoped for at the moment.

While Sticky was on the ground in misery with his injured arm, the car's ignition started, and Trevor heard a third shot fired, this time noticing a stream of water spewing from the vehicle's radiator. The shots were coming from that low knoll, and Trevor suddenly realized who was doing the shooting. No doubt it had been Mackenzie who'd followed them to where Malone's people were waiting, and was now doing what he could to disable the car.

The sound of screeching tires stirred the peace on the quiet street, and the Lincoln jetted backwards a hundred feet as if racing to beat bullets, suddenly slid to a stop, then spun a one-eighty turn and sped off down the road. Trevor knew they wouldn't get far with those holes in the radiator.

"About time you showed up," he said under his breath, thinking about Mackenzie. And then he turned around and started running in the direction from which he had come, down the railroad tracks toward the meeting bridge. He hoped to reach his van before Mackenzie caught up with him. He wasn't ready for a reunion with his sister just yet. And he wasn't ready to give up his endeavor for which he'd sacrificed so much. His sister finding him would surely add complications to his already complicated life, and the time for that was going to have to be later.

Before reaching the bridge he hurriedly searched the bushes in the area where he remembered tossing his pistol. He strained to remember which clump of weeds it appeared to land in, desperately hoping to find it to prevent it from being found by juveniles who would only get into trouble with it.

He became increasingly frustrated when he didn't find it right away, but he just couldn't leave it there for kids to find. He knew that Mackenzie would be this side of the knoll already, fast closing the gap between them. But he didn't look up to see where he was. He kept his focus on his search.

Suddenly, and almost accidentally while his hands were sweeping through the tall grass, his fingers found the smooth cool steel of the gun in a spot where he didn't actually expect to find it. Without looking back, he shoved it into its holster and sprinted as fast as he could toward the trail that led away from the tracks and up to the road where his van was parked. He had no idea how far behind Mackenzie was at this point. He guessed not very far at all.

And his guess was right. As he jumped into his van and started the engine, Del had reached the edge of the road less than a hundred yards away. Before the vehicle had time to speed away out of sight, Del managed to drop to his elbows with his 35mm camera out and quickly zoom focused on the van, snapping a total of four still shots.

It had been a crazy sequence of events, but Trevor and Del were both lucky, and each knew it. Del rolled onto one side and pulled his gear bag close where he could look inside. He stuffed his camera away, and put his headset back on his head, hoping Wendy was within a quarter of a mile, so he could talk to her. He spoke into the microphone, but he didn't hear any response. She was probably closer to a half mile away—outside the transmission range of their radios. He got back onto his feet and started back toward that other road where his car was parked, where Wendy watched anything that moved with the binoculars.

During the trip back to her apartment, he explained the details of what had happened. She grabbed his shoulder bag and reached inside, removed the little film can and placed it to her lips, kissing it. In her apartment she had converted part of her laundry room into a film developing dark room, and the two of them spent the balance of the afternoon developing his roll of film and studying the pictures. She had her own camera with her in the car at the bridge, in case she found anything interesting with the binoculars, but she never saw anything worth filming.

Del, on the other hand, had been snapping shots of nearly everything he was witness to during his adventure, including Trevor, Sticky, the Lincoln, some of the men in the Lincoln, and finally, Trevor's van. Many of his shots were close ups. When he wasn't running through the bushes or ventilating radiators with his .38 Super, he was shooting photos. He realized that his career choice would require a lot of that type of activity. It was all part of the deal.

"At least now we know for certain that he drives a van," Del remarked, drawing Wendy's attention to the photograph he'd taken showing Trevor climbing into his vehicle, "and it looks every bit as custom as I had expected. Note the unique shape of the roof, and that weird antenna. Shouldn't be too hard to identify if we spot it again. Now, if only we could find a way to predict where he'll be next."

"Good work, Del," she commended, staring sentimentally at one of the close ups of Trevor's face that Del had taken down by the tracks. He was almost impossible to recognize in that photo. Almost. But Wendy could see her brother behind his disguise, and she knew it was really him.

Del had been putting the puzzle together for her, and it appeared to be almost complete. From his photos they would be able to read the van's license plate, and Del's friends in the Department would be able to run a trace on it, to find out what alias the vehicle was registered under. From there they would also be able to find his residence address and other useful information. The trick for Del would be gathering the information he wanted without tipping off the police, who were also very interested in finding Trevor Luppert. But Del seemed to always find a way around those kinds of obstacles.

Meanwhile, Trevor, suspecting that his van had been seen by Del, decided to devote the balance of the afternoon to eavesdropping on Wendy and her detective, to determine exactly what they knew. He wasn't really surprised to learn they had photos of him, and of his van. He knew he should have expected that. Mackenzie was as good a detective as anyone was likely to find, and probably a cut above most. But he hadn't expected him to progress as quickly on the case as he was.

And now Trevor would be forced to abandon his first alias, destroy that particular driver's license, clean out the apartment rented under that name, switch the plates on his van to his second set registered under his second alias, and assume his new identity. He would have to be thorough. Mackenzie was on his trail and moving fast.

He also decided that it would be safer to change the color of the van. The current common white could be changed to an equally inconspicuous, generic shade of gray. He knew several good auto body shops, but he didn't want to involve anybody else. He decided to buy a case of gray spray paint and do the job himself. With a careful masking job and the right spray technique, he ended up with a decent looking paint job, by his standards, anyway.

And he changed his physical appearance yet again. Mackenzie would be looking for a long, dark haired, bearded man with glasses, normally wearing a baseball cap, as he did at the bridge. So Trevor decided to keep his bushy mustache but shave the beard, lose the sunglasses and baseball cap, and dye his hair blond. Nobody would be expecting to find a blond Trevor Luppert. And he would start wearing a western-style hat most of the time, to attain the urban cowboy look.

Malone wouldn't be giving up his hunt for the Vigilante. He wouldn't have any clear explanation about what occurred near the bridge, but that wouldn't stop him. He was the kind of man who would be obsessed with getting any problems out of his way, and he wouldn't let up until he was confident the job was done. Given the nature of his street enterprises, a vigilante presented a serious problem for him. And if he believed there were two of them working together, the problem's urgency would seem even greater.

Now that Malone's best hope for capturing the Vigilante had been substantially hindered, he could be expected to react severely against those around him whom he depended on for the successful execution of the task. And everyone who knew him knew how cruel and vicious he could be. There was certainly no envy for those sent to do Malone's work returning empty-handed, especially now.

But Trevor wasn't going to be able to help them. The danger they were in was part of what everyone bargained for when accepting a job working for Malone. And they wouldn't have hesitated administering his brutality if they had had the opportunity. The same went for Sticky. He'd dug his own grave.

Trevor realized he had to get back to focusing on his original mission, which had more to do with stopping bad people from harming good people than anything else. He was confident that he had successfully thrown everyone off his trail, at least for a while, and he would now be nearly as free to operate as he had ever been since starting this whole thing. He was thinking nearly, because even though Mackenzie shouldn't have any usable leads, he was proving to be quite a good detective, and he wasn't giving up. Trevor knew that Wendy wouldn't let him.

Del and Wendy followed the information trail they had, and learned pretty quickly that Trevor had already changed his alias. The apartment was empty. The bank account had been closed out. Trevor had once again vanished, seemingly into thin air. Their most encouraging lead thus far yielded nothing, and Del started wondering if he had reached a dead end in the game, with no viable strategy remaining. Of course, he'd had that feeling before. It didn't always mean very much.

Somehow Trevor must have known they were on his trail, Del was thinking. That was certainly how he acted near the bridge after the bullets started flying—almost as if he expected Del, or somebody else besides Malone's people, to be at the scene watching everything as it happened. And he hurried back to his van like he believed somebody was on his trail. And then he immediately changed his alias.

But how would he know he was under surveillance? And why would he expect to be? Del wasn't able to make any sense of it. Trevor *couldn't* know Del and Wendy were on his trail. There would be no way he could, unless…

Suddenly it hit him. And it was as if the proverbial light bulb had just been switched on inside his head. It should have been obvious all along that Trevor would be watching his sister. That would fit perfectly with his personality as Wendy described him, and would certainly be consistent with everything she told Del about Trevor's preoccupation with her safety.

Del's mind began stirring with all sorts of crazy thoughts. It all made perfect sense now, and it would explain a lot of things. Trevor was certainly a skilled and clever spy. That was the focus of his life, and he had invented an array of special tools to help him do it. Now that he was thinking about it, Del wondered why he hadn't considered it before. And he wondered how long Trevor had been spying on them. How much would he know? Would he know that the police now wanted him for suspicion of murder?

Del figured his guess had to be right. Trevor must have been spying on him and Wendy. There would be no other logical reason for him to go to the trouble of changing his alias. And what about the van Del snapped photos of? Trevor could surely be expected to do something about that. It would be too easy to recognize, with its unusual top.

The big question Del couldn't avoid at this point was what he should do about it. He could conduct a careful sweep of Wendy's apartment, as well as his own, for microphones. He could do the same with their cars. If he got lucky enough to find them all, he could certainly hinder Trevor's ability to spy on them. Of course, if he did that, Trevor would know they had figured out his program. And that could only make him more elusive. There could be no gain in cutting the only link between them that currently existed. The dilemma would be figuring out just how to make use of that link, such as it was.

And then, the other question Del started considering was whether or not he should inform Wendy of his suspicion. If he decided that he should, he would have to figure out when, where, and how, so as to avoid alerting Trevor. And they would have to work out some kind of system for communicating, like a code that Trevor wouldn't detect. That could be a real trick, all right. But if he didn't tell her exactly what was going on, it might make things even more complicated.

For the time being, or at least until he figured out some way to inform Wendy, Del decided to simply keep this knowledge to himself and pretend like he didn't know what Trevor was up to. Maybe that would be the best strategy. Perhaps the longer Trevor spied on them, the better their chances of eventually catching up with him. It seemed like a good theory, anyway. Del decided to continue his investigation as if he had no idea anyone was eavesdropping on him. He didn't want to risk tipping off Trevor.

He could search his own place for the hidden bugs to verify his theory, quietly and discreetly without raising any red flags. If he found any, he could presume Wendy's apartment was also bugged. And he couldn't ignore his own need to know for certain, even though he realized there would be no way to know just when, and from where Trevor was listening to them.

CHAPTER VII

When the authorities finally announced publicly that they were looking for Trevor Luppert in connection with the shooting death of the man who had been charged with multiple rapes and later cleared of the charges against him, his name and face were once again in the media. And the missing millionaire mystery was a whole lot more interesting to everyone this time around.

Wendy's apartment was suddenly under twenty-four hour police surveillance. Del recognized the unmarked cars parked down the street. And the day right after he spotted them, he noticed they were watching him as well. He couldn't drive anywhere without being followed.

When he spoke to Walter Collier again, he learned that Luppert Systems had received new visits from law enforcement people. And media reporters were starting to hound the employees more aggressively than they previously had when news first broke of Trevor's disappearance.

Del could only speculate how the renewed public obsession was influencing Trevor's strategies. He knew that it could only make him more cautious, and more difficult to find. And there would be a lot more competition out there for anybody trying to find him.

Everything would be different now. Sure, it seemed to Del that he had actually come close to meeting up with Trevor, but that was all he could say about it. And, again he reminded himself, close wasn't getting the job done. It wasn't what Wendy had hired him for. She wanted to meet with and talk to her brother, and that was why she hired Del. As attractive as she was, he needed to keep his focus on the job.

He found himself being awakened by the buzzing of his doorbell, interrupting whatever nonsensical dream he was having. He glanced at the alarm clock on his nightstand and noticed that it was not quite two o'clock in the morning.

"Who could that possibly be?" he mumbled to himself, trying to imagine why anyone would be at his door at that dark hour. He wanted to roll over and go back to sleep, and he felt tired enough, but he was also too curious to ignore it. Besides, the doorbell kept buzzing. Somebody sure was persistent.

In less than a minute he was out of bed and two-thirds dressed, and he grabbed up his .38 Super off his dresser and disengaged the thumb safety. It wasn't always safe to answer one's apartment door at weird hours when the rest of the world was asleep, at least in Los Angeles. He had no desire to meet some dangerous crazy person there without his gun in his hand. For all he knew, whoever it was might try to force his way into Del's apartment—maybe try to stab him or shoot him. It couldn't hurt to be prepared for whatever awaited him at his door.

And he quietly approached the door from one side, along the wall, and asked who was there. It seemed longer than it probably really was before he heard an answer, but as soon as he heard Wendy's voice, he realized his precautions were probably no longer necessary.

"You're out there by yourself?" he asked her, then listened carefully for how she answered.

"No, I brought my big brother along to protect me," she responded sarcastically, "Of course I'm by myself, silly. Who else is going to get up in the middle of the night to escort me to your apartment? I've been in your apartment, Del, and I wouldn't say it's that exciting. So are you going to let me in, or what?"

He un-cocked the pistol and set it under his coffee table where she wouldn't see it and think he was paranoid, then opened the door, "Yeah, sure. Please come in. Just wanted to make sure you were alone, that's all. So, what brings you here at almost two o'clock in the morning?"

She stepped inside, and he closed the door.

"I couldn't sleep. There is all this stuff in the news about Trevor and everything. I don't know. I can't seem to get it out of my mind. Do you think it's true what they're saying? Do you believe he murdered that man?"

Del cleared his throat, "Not exactly. I don't think 'murder' is the right word. It looks like he shot the man to stop him from raping and possibly killing that girl, but that's not murder. That's *preventing* murder, the way I see it."

She wrapped her arms around his torso and pressed her face against his chest.

"What are we going to do?" she asked despairingly, "What do you think Trevor is going to do?"

"Gosh, if I knew that, then maybe I'd be closer to finding him for you. I wish I *could* predict every move your brother made. I'd be a much better detective than I am now."

She shook her head, "No. You're a fine detective now. My brother is just impossible. He's always been impossible. I don't know why I can't simply let him go, get him out of my life the way he wants me to. But I just can't. I can't."

"I doubt he would want that," Del remarked, "Not completely, anyway. I would bet money you're not out of his life. At least, you're not absent from his thoughts. I'm almost sure of it."

She didn't comment, but her silence told Del she was thinking about what he said. He knew it was the truth, and more importantly, it was what she needed to hear right then. Her arms squeezed tightly around his body.

Del and Wendy spent the next couple of days trying to find clever ways to avoid contact with reporters, and elude the discreet but almost constant police surveillance, which was becoming quite a challenge. Wendy was finding it almost unbearably annoying, and Del found it next to impossible to continue his investigative work effectively under such scrutiny.

The two of them finally decided to take a short vacation together, to get out of the Los Angeles area for a little while. They both realized that it was a much needed break, and they went for a drive up to the Oregon coast.

Del was also glad to be getting away from Trevor's eavesdropping for awhile, after finally finding a Lupport microphone in his own apartment at the end of his exhaustive search. He left it alone when he discovered it, so that Trevor wouldn't know he had discovered it. And he still hadn't mentioned anything to Wendy about it.

The worst part about knowing he had a bug around was that he never knew when Trevor was tuned in, and when he wasn't. He just had to assume that the eavesdropping was going on all the time. His conversations with Wendy would have to sound natural, but at the same time, he was careful about what he talked about. And no matter how he tried to ignore it, he couldn't prevent it from affecting his relationship with Trevor's sister to some extent.

They would be escaping that for a little while, anyway. Trevor might follow them up to Oregon if he was that obsessed with keeping tabs on them, but he wouldn't be able to listen in on them all the time. There would be no way for him to know ahead of time which hotel or hotel room they were going to be staying in, so it was safe to assume it wouldn't be bugged. And even though he had invented a device for listening through walls, there was every reason to believe he didn't possess a working model.

But Trevor wasn't interested in leaving Los Angeles right then. There was too much work to be done there still, and he sensed that his time for getting it done was now clearly limited.

And lately he had been closely watching a couple of ex-cons who had been recently released from prison on early parole. They were cousins, and they had been serving time for the same crime; attempted kidnapping, a crime in which they had conspired together before their scheme was derailed.

Trevor decided to monitor their behavior for awhile to make certain their new freedom would be accepted as a second chance for two reformed and grateful men, eager to return to society and earn an honest living. But it wasn't long at all until the two began planning another kidnapping, this time determined to avoid the same mistakes that landed them in jail the first time. They were planning everything more carefully this time around.

When Trevor intercepted some of their communications revealing their new plans, he intensified his spying activities. He needed to know who they intended to kidnap, exactly how they planned to do it, when they planned to do it, and where. He planted bugs everywhere he expected them to spend time, tapped into their phone lines, and broke into their computer files. Whenever they left their apartments, he knew about it, and he tracked their movements. He had them wired every way from Sunday, and recorded every word they spoke.

He learned they were getting financial support from their aunt, and therefore neither of them were working or even looking for a job. This left them free all day every day to mastermind their plot. And they began spending nearly every waking moment planning the job.

Both were convinced that the only reason they botched their first kidnapping attempt and ended up in prison was because they hadn't worked out the details well enough beforehand. It was simply a matter of poor planning. They weren't going to make the same mistake again. And it couldn't have been more convenient for Trevor, who was able to follow their scheme to the last detail using his various spy tools.

Soon he knew *who* they planned to abduct; the rich mayor's three-year old daughter. They were watching the girl's mother closely. Their plan was to watch and wait for the perfect opportunity to snatch the girl, who went everywhere with her mother.

After studying the mother's regular routine for several weeks, they knew which department stores she shopped in, and they studied the floor plans of each while noting the positions of the video cameras, where all the doors and exits were located, and they rehearsed their operation. Wearing a disguise, one of the kidnapers would have the job of distracting the mother while the other would grab the girl. It would require perfect timing when the opportunity presented itself, and they would have to move with mechanical precision. There would be no room for error this time. Getting caught would mean going to prison for life no doubt, with likely no possibility for parole after a second conviction. They didn't like talking about the possibility of getting caught again. Instead, they rehearsed their operation, over and over.

And Trevor listened from his van parked at a nearby location where it wouldn't be noticed. He'd done his homework, too, and had learned quite a bit about the mayor's wife and daughter, as well as about the cousins plotting the kidnapping.

Eventually he had enough of the cousins' conversations recorded that if he were to send a tape to the police, the crime would surely be prevented. But a recording of a communication between two parties, recorded without the knowledge or consent of either party, detailing a crime that wasn't yet actually committed, sent to the authorities from an anonymous source, may not have a lot of leverage for getting these predators out of society. This particular crime could be avoided all right, but what about the next, and the one after that?

Trevor realized that the cousins needed to get caught in the act. They needed to be put away forever, or they would continue finding ways to prey on others. He needed to help them become entangled in their own web of treachery. He needed to trap them in a sting operation. The police had the resources to do it, but their priorities would be on other things. The whole deal was up to him, and he accepted the responsibility of it without hesitation. He had the resources, tools, time, will and determination to put a permanent end to their criminal careers.

He was conscious of the fact that he was the only one currently watching their activities, and that if not for him, these guys could possibly execute their crime undetected. They might actually get away with it, and inevitably move on to other, equally sinister crimes. They would eventually get caught at some point probably, but they could sure harm a lot of innocent people in the meantime. Trevor was determined to not allow that to happen.

When they snatched the child away from her mother, the mayor's wife was too preoccupied with her shopping to notice until after they had the girl gagged and into the car they had waiting right outside the store. When she finally realized her daughter was missing, she frantically searched every corner of the store and almost immediately called the police on her cell phone. She was noticeably and understandably distraught, and frustrated by the fact that nobody in the store reported seeing anything unusual.

Trevor had been observing the entire sequence of events, and wanted to put her mind at ease by letting her know that he had the situation under control, but he knew he didn't dare. Doing that could jeopardize his objective. He had to let the cousins carry out their crime to its full extent in order to set the noose of his snare. It was the way he had it planned, though it seemed risky. But he decided there was really no other way to do it properly.

He'd been monitoring a number of others with criminal records before the cousins had conceived this kidnapping plot, but once he discovered what they were up to, he started focusing on their activities almost around the clock. He had the tools for it. Whenever he needed to sleep, he could record everything picked up by his hidden microphones for playback later. The Luppert microphones were so small, it was unlikely that any unsuspecting subject would ever find one without knowing exactly what to look for. Trevor had also spent a lot of time and research in determining the best places to plant them, and he knew how to use them effectively, together with some of his other gadgets. The cousins never even had a clue they were under surveillance.

The kidnapers had the important details carefully worked out this time around. They would make contact with the girl's parents by mail, because it was too easy to trace telephone communications these days. They used printed letters cut out of the *Los Angeles Times* and pasted to their custom ransom note, to avoid using traceable handwriting. They handled everything wearing gloves to avoid leaving fingerprints. And they gave clear instructions about when, where, and how to find the next instructions, leading to additional instructions about when, where, and how to make the payoff. And of course, the family was warned not to involve the police. But it was presumed they would, anyway. The mayor's wife had already called them before she left the department store. They were working on trying to find the girl well before the ransom note was received. But they had no idea about where to look for the kidnapers.

The predictability of events was almost unsettling. Something didn't seem quite right. Everything was too simple. The cousins would carry out their scheme of extortion and walk right into Trevor's trap in the process. They would go to jail. Things were rarely that easy in this line of work.

And then everything suddenly changed. He heard them now discussing what they planned to do with the little girl, and it turned his strategy upside down. He was horrified to learn that they had no intentions at this point of handing the girl over safely to her parents. Because she might be able to identify them, they started planning how they would get rid of her. Trevor never expected that this could be part of their scheme. It completely caught him off guard. It certainly wasn't part of their original plan.

He couldn't allow this game to continue. A little girl's life was in serious danger, and it had to be stopped immediately. Trevor strapped on the holster for his Browning 9mm and started his van. The time had come for a rescue action, and getting the girl safely out of the place was his first priority. He was ready to use force to accomplish it if it came to that. He'd shoot those cousins dead in their tracks without hesitation, if it prevented them from harming the girl.

But by the time he quietly entered the premises through the unguarded laundry room door, they were gone. And he discovered pretty quickly that they had taken the girl away.

They had taken her, gagged, tied up, and blindfolded in a gunnysack, to a secluded and neglected avocado orchard, where they planned to strangle her with a length of cable and then bury her in a three-foot deep hole. They decided to take turns digging, and then flip a coin to determine who would have the unpleasant task of tightening the cable around the girl's neck.

They both wanted to conclude the dirty deed as rapidly as possible and get out of the area before anybody saw them. One kept watch while the other hastily shoveled dirt out of the ground, and then they switched roles for two or three minutes, and continued the process until they had a large enough hole excavated for their purpose.

A coin was then tossed, and one of them grabbed a piece of cable from their kit and proceeded to untie the gunnysack in order to expose the girl's neck.

The cross hairs of a riflescope were centered over his forehead, and a finger tip had begun applying steady pressure on the trigger when suddenly loud shouting erupted in the area closely surrounding the cousins. Uniformed police were emerging from the trees with their guns drawn, and the cousins' surrendering hands went up over their heads. The police aggressively approached them from multiple directions and apprehended them before they had a chance to run or resist.

Trevor gave a sigh of relief. He was able to avoid pulling the trigger this time to save the victim. He had called the police in the course of tracking the cousins to the orchard, and directed them to the precise location. And he had hoped for, but not expected them to arrive in time to stop a tragedy. He was completely ready to stop it himself if they couldn't make it, but they went a long ways toward restoring his confidence in their capabilities on this day. He thought about it for a moment. He might be more inclined to help them fight crime from now on, and try to work with them, rather than working entirely alone as he'd been doing until now.

But he would think more about that later. Right now he had to find a secret path to lead him out of the orchard. He was still a wanted man by the authorities, and there were currently a growing number of them swarming the orchard and working to secure the area as a crime scene. He was well camouflaged at the moment, wearing his custom ghillie sniper suit made by tying hundreds of earth-tone colored strands of burlap to a full-body jump suit covered with netting. He looked just like a mound of weeds. And he was in thick brush. If he could keep completely still, he should be able to remain undetected indefinitely. But if they brought in dogs, or if they suspected he was in the area, staying hidden could be especially difficult. At the moment there wasn't much he could do. He was barely eighty yards away from the crime scene. If he moved at all, he would risk drawing someone's attention to his position. And there were a lot of police in the area now.

He could stay put for awhile without moving a muscle easily enough, but he started worrying about his van. It was parked less than a quarter of a mile away, and pretty soon there would be a lot of news media people in the area, and the police would be taking a hard look at everything they found. It might stick out like a sore thumb. Surely they would be checking out every vehicle parked within a certain radius of the orchard.

He concentrated on breathing quietly and avoiding any twitches or sudden movements. He stayed low to the ground lying on top of his rifle, and that made him more difficult to spot, but he couldn't see much of what was going on. He could only try to listen and estimate exactly where the police were poking around looking for clues. This would be another close one, if he got out of there undetected.

There wasn't anything he could do about his van right now. If they found it, they found it. Currently there would be no way for him to move without being seen. He'd have parked farther away if there'd been more time, but saving the girl's life was his first priority when he arrived, and he had no way of knowing how much time he would ultimately have.

He was able to relax some now knowing that the girl was finally safe. Even if the police discovered him here, the girl had been rescued from a horrible fate, and that was worth all the risk. He was also confident that if it hadn't been for his efforts, the girl would be dead, and her murderers may well have gotten away with this crime. His own activities, although sometimes illegal, saved lives. He wondered how much consideration a court of law would give him on that when he was finally caught. Hopefully if he remained still and quiet long enough, that wouldn't be today.

And so he remained in the same position until after dark, when he could move out without being noticed, and he finally got back to his van. It appeared not to have been tampered with, much to his relief. The police had apparently focused on the cousins' car, which had been parked on a nearby but different street. Another close call, Trevor was thinking, but he was still free to operate...For now. He couldn't help wondering how much longer he would continue to elude everyone. It was getting more challenging now. That much was certain. But there was still a lot of work left for him to do, and he wouldn't be able to quit as long as he knew his efforts continued to effectively stop crime.

CHAPTER VIII

After two weeks of vacation, Del and Wendy returned to Los Angeles. Things had settled down a little bit seemingly, but not a lot. There was still a manhunt in progress for the Vigilante, now publicly identified as the missing millionaire, Trevor Luppert. And anyone and everyone associated with Trevor in any way was sought after for insight or information to his whereabouts.

When Trevor learned that his sister and Del were back home from their trip, he resumed his spying on them. But now he would listen in on them only periodically, because he had plenty of other work to do, and his crime fighting was his first priority. It was the central purpose of his life at this point.

Del knew that Trevor would be watching him. He also knew that the police were watching him, and watching Wendy especially, hoping that one of them would lead to Trevor. But even though the police wanted Trevor in connection with the killing they suspected he was involved in, they were also very conscious of the fact that he was regularly providing them with valuable information and helping them solve crimes.

Trevor was progressively making himself a valuable asset to the police. And they began to realize that he was able to do quite a lot that they couldn't, because his methods weren't restricted by their rules, and his technology was in many ways superior to what they could access on the department's budget. It became part of his strategy for his own survival.

If they needed his help out there in the streets, he reasoned, they'd be less inclined to focus on apprehending him. And it was good logic, as far as the politics of an organization would accommodate. But he knew he'd have to be careful not to let his guard down.

One of the things about the Luppert monitoring system that made it so convenient was its impulse selector grid. Each tiny hidden microphone would be assigned a number that corresponded with its own unique series of impulse signals that the receiver recognized, distinguishing each particular bug by its number. The selector grid allowed Trevor to have hundreds of microphones planted in different locations, each logged into the unit's data bank with its location description. From his van he could tune in to any of them and switch back and forth between the numbered microphones for listening just as fast as he could enter their numbers on his touch pad. And he could listen to two separate bugs simultaneously if he wanted, or to one or two while recording the transmission from either or both, because the system had twin receivers and twin recording machines. He controlled everything with a touch pad, and could read the microphones' location descriptions on the system's screen.

He had microphones hidden in restaurants, parking lots, alleyways, bus stations, phone booths, offices, public rest rooms, under bridges, in parks, and in numerous other locations where he believed he might intercept useful information. And he continued to expand his database and monitoring field. He eventually learned which locations were active, and which weren't. His database continued to evolve.

But with the recent media attention focusing on the Vigilante, finally exposed as Trevor Luppert, he didn't think it would be safe to continue meeting with his street contacts for information. It seemed a lot safer now just to avoid them altogether. He wasn't relying on them lately as much as he was previously, anyway, and since that little episode with Sticky, he didn't feel he could trust most of them. Mingling with that element that dwelt in the streets would simply be too risky at this point.

But he'd already collected enough information about the criminal world in Southern California to keep himself busy for awhile. He was able to access a list of felons scheduled for parole or recently released, and the investigation work was immense. But as much as he was able to thwart local criminal activity, there was always an awful lot of it going on that escaped him, and he was well aware of that.

He was already starting to rotate the micro video cameras, because he had such a limited supply of those. If he hadn't left his company when he did, he would have had access to more tools, and right now he realized he could sure use more. The sound restoring/thermal viewing device would be especially useful. If he'd stayed around just a little while longer, he could have had it to use now. He considered his schematic to be mostly theoretical, however, and didn't expect his company to be able to assemble a working model as soon as they did. He hadn't considered it quite ready for production just yet, and judging by Del's field test, he was probably right. The device still needed a bit of tinkering.

He still had the Selective Ear to play with, and he found it extremely useful in certain applications. With it, he could listen to a low-level conversation from more than two hundred yards away, just by aiming it at the individuals talking. It could isolate two people speaking in a crowd and block out most of the surrounding noise. The key to its effectiveness was its extremely sensitive unidirectional microphone. Trevor's product was a refinement of the best military-grade models that he'd spent the better part of a year studying and experimenting with.

But staying with his company much longer wouldn't have allowed him the time and freedom to operate that this job demanded, and so he decided that he had to make the change when he did. He had no regrets about that. And he realized that he was able to accomplish quite a lot with the tools he had. The amount of crime he was able to expose was keeping him busier than he'd ever been in his life. And unlike before, now he felt that his life had a real purpose.

He soon discovered that Wendy's and Del's relationship had seemingly grown into something during their time together in Oregon. They were now working together almost completely in their search for Trevor Luppert. And he couldn't avoid noticing that they worked well together. As far as he could tell, they seemed to be a good match, though he hated to think of his baby sister as all grown up. It made him kind of sad in a way, because it was one more thing that seemed to separate him from his youth.

His task of spying on Del and Wendy was losing its priority for now, Trevor kept reminding himself. He was too busy with other concerns to be devoting much time to monitoring them. And he was pretty confident they didn't have any immediate leads on him.

What he really wanted to do was find an effective way to spy on Leo Malone, the undisputed leader of organized crime in the region. Since Malone found those microphones in his office, his security could be expected to be tightened up quite a bit. And knowing there was a vigilante around intercepting his profits would make him want to really focus his attention on the problem. That last meeting with Sticky was evidence enough for Trevor of Malone's obsession. But things could be even more dangerous now, since the news releases linking the Vigilante with Trevor Luppert. Now Malone would know who he was hunting, even if that knowledge wouldn't lead him directly to Trevor.

Planting more surveillance devices in Malone's domain was no longer a viable option under the present circumstances. Trevor might actually be able to do it successfully, but it would be simply too risky even for him. He needed some way in which he could spy on him safely, from a distance. The Selective Ear was good for when Malone was out in the open, such as when he went to play golf as he'd been known to occasionally do. But it didn't pick up conversations through walls. He needed the sound restoring technology for that.

But the S.R.T.V. (Sound Restoring Thermal Viewing) device that he had designed himself wasn't available to him now. It was locked away securely at Luppert Systems, protected under the same sophisticated security alarms that he also developed himself.

The idea crossed his mind on more than one occasion that he could break into the vault and "borrow" the device, at least for a while. He previously rejected the idea due to the risky aspects of returning to the one place where people might expect to find him more than any other. The company was undoubtedly under constant police surveillance and government scrutiny lately, and getting in and out of there could be tricky. He knew as well as anyone the strengths and weaknesses of the alarm system, and he still had his keys to the key locks and numbers to the combination locks. They likely hadn't changed those since he left. He knew the premises, and the routines of the Luppert security guards. He could get in and out without being detected if he planned it right. It would be tricky, but he could do it.

The whole idea of breaking and entering at his own company, and sneaking out with company property, was not one that appealed to him very much. But when he thought about how useful that particular piece of equipment would be in spying on Leo Malone, he knew he had to consider it. And the more he thought about it, the more he started contemplating exactly how he might execute such an operation, if he decided to actually attempt it. Even before making any decision, he had the operation carefully calculated in his head, down to the smallest detail.

His need to know what Malone was up to put him over the fence on it, and he made an inconspicuous survey of the whole area surrounding the company property during daylight, assessing the level of surveillance. His plan was to go in at 2:00 a.m., because that would be the time of least activity. There would be a security guard on duty, but no other employees around at that time of morning.

The hardest part would be getting past the night shift security guard, Howard Nims. Trevor knew Howard well. He personally hired him three years ago, and he knew him to be a perceptive and conscientious employee. Not too many things got past Howard.

But Trevor knew Howard's regular routine, and he knew when he made his periodic rounds to inspect things, and precisely where he would be at any given time. It had all been recorded in the night shift logbook, which Trevor had examined many times. There wasn't much deviation to Howard's routine, and that was probably his only weakness as a security guard.

At precisely five to two each morning, Howard left the security office where a dozen monitor screens showed video coverage of almost every space within the property, and walked around inspecting things to keep himself awake. His route generally consumed about twenty-five minutes, give or take five. Trevor's estimated available time frame was fifteen minutes, because Howard usually reached the vault area right about five after two. Trevor would want to be completely off the premises by the time Howard returned to the monitor room. *If everything went according to plan, he would need only fifteen minutes.*

He dressed in a black athletic jump suit and rubbed dark brown leather dye into his silent moccasins, to help them blend well into the shadows. When the hour approached, he pulled a dark ski mask over his head, and with his gear bag slung over his shoulder by its strap, he skulked up to the tall chain link fence out of the darkness at a spot he'd determined was hidden from all surveillance. In less than a minute he was safely up and over, carefully avoiding injury on the top strands of barbed wire.

He was able to move about the premises with stealth and precision, every step according to his careful prior calculations, and he reached the storage vault exactly on schedule. Circumventing the alarms proved easier than anticipated. He carried each individual key in a separate pocket and he'd memorized which was which, so as to avoid the sound of keys jingling together in one pocket, and also to shorten the time spent searching for each key.

When he set his eyes on the device he came for, he couldn't help feeling excited. They hadn't deviated much at all from his plans, at least externally, from its general appearance. It looked very much as he had envisioned the final product would look. He knew the real proof of his invention would come in the testing, and he could hardly wait to try it out for himself.

But first he'd have to get off the company premises without being detected, and he could feel his heart suddenly racing when he heard the sound of somebody quietly approaching the vault. Damn his timing, he thought. He glanced at his watch to see how much he might have miscalculated. According to that he hadn't miscalculated at all. It was almost eight minutes past two, and Howard's regular routine had him leaving the vault area before that, having checked things out there by five after.

Trevor was right on schedule. Maybe Howard had varied his routine. Maybe all the big changes with the company lately threw him off his regular routine he had established over the past three years. Certainly many of the employees' routines had been disrupted by recent events. Or maybe somebody at the company expected him to come around for the latest product, assuming he knew it existed.

There were plenty of maybes to consider. But presently, about the only option for him was to freeze like a statue behind the vault door and hold his breath. And as much as he tried to listen to the sounds outside the door, it wasn't easy to hear anything over the thumping of his own heartbeat.

His anticipation suddenly simmered with the sight of Corduroy, the company cat. Corduroy lived on the property, and went exploring nightly. On more than one occasion, he tripped the alarm during his adventures, and each time Trevor received a phone call from the police in the middle of the night, notifying him of the incident. Corduroy was a poor substitute for a guard dog, obviously, but everyone at the company seemed to like cats, and not everyone was fond of dogs, especially attack dogs.

Trevor was greatly relieved to discover that the noise he heard was made by a cat and not a security guard, and he reached down to scratch the animal's ears when he remembered what he had come for. There wasn't much time. He grabbed the unit off the shelf and then locked the vault back up, making sure Corduroy wasn't inside when he locked it.

Just as he intended, he made it safely past the alarms and over the fence before Howard would have most likely returned to the monitor room.

When he had reached the privacy of his van, he was able to examine the device more closely. The more he played around with it, the more he liked it. He realized it had some deficiencies, but nothing that couldn't be ironed out with a little trial and error. Overall he was pleased with it, and he knew it would work well for his purpose.

His next order of business would be scouting out the streets around Leo Malone's office, to find a place from which he could use this device just the way Del had done. He needed to find a position where he could aim the unit directly into the office without having to look through more than one wall, floor, or window. It didn't penetrate more than one barrier very well at all. A place where he could park his van would be ideal, as long as it wouldn't be too conspicuous.

The early morning hours were a good time to check things out because nobody was around to notice him. He hoped he wouldn't see any police cars. The police tend to get curious when they see people out and about at three o'clock in the morning. His van was unusual enough that it might draw somebody's attention. Trevor kept watch for police cars, but luckily didn't see any.

Depending on how busy that part of town was later, there should be a place to park his van somewhere across the street, probably close to where Del had parked when he had his own opportunity to test the equipment.

Trevor knew Malone's office well after having breached his security and having explored the inside several times when the crime leader was still unsuspecting. He knew exactly where to aim the viewer for best results. He decided to go catch five or six hours of sleep and come back later when Malone would be in, and there would be plenty of other cars parked on the street among which his van could sit inconspicuously, and he could do his business without drawing any attention.

When he returned at a quarter to ten, he found the best parking spots already taken. He finally found an available space within viewing range of Malone's office, and parked his van there as if he had some regular business in one of the surrounding buildings.

From his van he could look inside any of the surrounding offices and listen to meetings in progress. This was by far the handiest device he had ever invented, he was certain. The images behind walls were anything but clearly defined, but they were images easily identifiable as people, and that was plenty good for what Trevor needed at the moment. And even more important than the visual images was the listening capability. That part of the technology was working perfectly.

Trevor was able to run the device off of his second vehicle battery with a special adapter, saving the unit's battery pack, and allowing him to operate the device for a longer duration than normally expected. Also, because all of the glass in his van was tinted, he could operate the device, which was somewhat similar in size to early model camcorders, without being noticed by anyone walking or driving by his van. He could spy in comfortable privacy.

The first hour of spying yielded nothing of significance. Leo Malone made a few phone calls, placed a bet on a closed-circuit televised boxing match, the outcome of which he no doubt intended to rig, and spent close to twenty minutes on the line with his accountant arguing tax matters. By the time he hung up he was in his characteristic hostile mood.

Then around eleven o'clock he received two of his henchmen into his office, and the conversation quickly drew to the subject of the Vigilante. Trevor's ears suddenly strained to hear every word, almost as if he'd been shocked awake out of a deep sleep.

He thought about the extraordinary scenario finding him listening to a conversation between the biggest criminal in Los Angeles and his hired guns, concerning a new lead on the Vigilante. What are the odds against that happening, he wondered? He wanted to hold his breath to listen to every word.

"Boss," one of them reported, "about the Vigilante; Victor and I found out where the girl lives, and where she spends a lot of time. And we've got the country house ready. We could hold her there for three weeks or longer if we need to."

"Let's hope we don't need her alive that long," Malone coldly responded, "And I presume you've got it all worked out as to when and where you'll pick her up?"

"It's all worked out, Boss."

"You've been busy. That's good, because I've seen too much incompetence lately. Maybe this time a job will get done right. Mr. Luppert will be coming to us when he finds out what we've got. He'll be angry, and he'll be worried. In other words, he'll be desperate and vulnerable. I've been waiting too long for that. And we'll be ready for him."

Malone then dismissed them from his office and placed a phone call to a nursing home back East to say Happy Birthday to his mother, like a son with a warm heart.

Trevor had heard everything he was going to hear on this day of any importance to him. And he contemplated what he'd just heard. The *girl* they were talking about had to be Wendy. Who else would he be so concerned about? Malone did his research. He knew the police believed the Vigilante was Trevor Luppert, and he'd learned that Trevor had a sister. That was the way Leo Malone operated. When he knew who the family members or loved ones were, he used them. And he would harm them if it served his purpose, or have them killed. And the worst part about it was that he would enjoy it.

This was something Trevor never planned on. If anything bad were to happen to his sister as a result of his own actions, he would never be able to forgive himself. But it was in fact the attempt made to kidnap her several years ago that really inspired his current occupation more than anything else. And the presence of danger from people like Malone made this whole struggle against crime seem more necessary. The risk factor had never been greater than it was right now, though, and there was no escaping that present reality.

There had been a frustrating vagueness to the exchange of words he had just heard. The Information was vital, but unfortunately short on details, and Trevor needed to know more. The important questions like when, where, and how, were given no answer. And the people working for Leo Malone…Trevor knew he wouldn't be able to protect Wendy properly if he didn't know exactly who he was protecting her from.

His first inclination was to hurry over to her apartment and warn her about the impending danger. But he didn't have to think about it very long before he realized very little if anything could be accomplished with that. His sister would surely think he was nuts. She likely already considered him more than a little bit paranoid, he thought. After all, he'd been living a most unusual life in recent months. If he suddenly showed up on her doorstep telling her that the Mafia were out to get her, she'd have to think he'd finally gone off the deep end.

Del knew about Malone, and about the kind of wicked criminal he was. But even Del might not fully grasp the essence of what the man was planning. At this point, a warning from

Trevor wouldn't be taken seriously enough, and even if it was, how could it make the situation go away? He knew he'd have to rely on another plan.

He knew a little bit about some of Malone's people. He'd done his homework before starting all of this, and he'd familiarized himself with Malone's operation. But there had been a lot of changes in his organization lately, and some of the people had already been replaced. Trevor didn't know anything about the one named Victor, and the voice of that other one didn't sound familiar. They must be the new recruits. Trevor couldn't help wondering how many new people Malone had hired on since all of this began.

He waited in his van and watched the building to see who exited the front door. He kept a digital camera with a zoom lens focused and ready. When two men finally stepped out he captured close-ups of their faces, and followed them to the car they climbed into. He recorded a close up of the license plate, and then started his van. He would follow their car and observe as much as he could.

The car didn't travel toward the same part of the city where Wendy's apartment was located. Of course, that only meant that their planned time for kidnapping her wasn't likely to be within the next couple of hours. But he wasn't even sure whether these men were indeed the same men who'd been in Malone's office a moment earlier. It was only reasonable to presume that they *probably* were, and right now that was the best he had to go on.

Trevor lost track of the car less than ten minutes later in the heavy mid-morning traffic, and wasn't able to find it again. He had hoped to be able to follow the car to the place alluded to in Malone's office, but there wasn't a country place that he was aware of near the area where he lost the car, and there were seemingly endless old farmhouses around the city. The location they intended to use could be any one of a thousand or more different locations. Given enough time, Trevor could find out exactly where they planned to hold Wendy, but he wasn't sure just how much time he had—probably not very much, anyway. Leo Malone was known to use a lot of different locations for his cocaine distribution, frequently changing sites to keep the authorities always guessing, and guessing incorrectly.

Trevor suddenly felt like he had lost control of the situation. With time on his side he would gain a handle on things. He could input the plate number of that car into his computer and retrieve data from the department of motor vehicles. He had the hacker skills to do it. And he would have a registered name, and do his background investigation from there. But that all took time, and he was guessing that he didn't have very much time at all. He remembered what was said in Malone's office; that they already had a plan in place for picking her up. It seemed like a pretty strong indication that there wasn't going to be very much time until they would grab her.

Trevor's thinking started shifting as to whether or not he should warn Wendy. Even if she didn't take it seriously, it might provide her with a tiny bit of awareness, and even the tiniest bit would be better than nothing. And maybe if he explained the whole situation to Del…The detective might get it. He was a smart one. They would have a chance to get prepared if they had the information. Maybe they could take another trip out of the city for awhile. That could make it next to impossible for someone like Malone to find her. The challenge might be convincing her to do it. Wendy was an independent woman who did what she wanted to do. Maybe Del would be able to convince her. Trevor just needed to convince Del. That might not be too difficult after all.

He turned off of the boulevard and started making his way back toward Wendy's apartment. He thought about how he was going to approach his sister after dodging her search efforts over the last several months. That might not be easy, but he knew he had to do it for her safety.

He switched on his receiver and entered the selection on the grid's touch pad to bring up the microphones in her apartment. In another twenty minutes he would be in the neighborhood.

CHAPTER IX

Wendy wasn't expecting any calls when her cell phone rang. Del was with her in her apartment. She could count all of those she had given that number to on one hand, and she rarely received calls from anyone other than Del.

Surprised, she reached into her purse and found the ringing phone, flicked it open and raised it to her ear.

"Hello," she said, then listened curiously to find out who would answer. She had been intending to order Caller ID service since she bought the new phone, but just hadn't gotten around to it yet with so many different distractions lately. In this case it wouldn't have revealed the identity of the caller, anyway.

"Wendy?" the unmistakable voice said.

"Trev, where are you, and why haven't you called sooner? I've been dying to talk to you about a lot of things lately."

"I know. Me too. But listen, Sis, I need you to do me a big favor. It's really important. Is your investigator friend with you now?"

She hesitated, looking at Del for guidance. He nodded.

"Yes, he's here. But he's not like everyone else who's looking for you. He's working for me."

"Yeah, I know. But I need to talk to him. Can you put him on the phone?"

She handed her cell phone over to Del, and he put it up to his hear with a surprised look on his face.

"This is Del," he said, sounding somewhat puzzled.

"Delmar Mackenzie," declared Trevor, "I know the two of us have never met, but we know each other. You've done your research on me, and I've certainly done my research about you."

"I'd say that would be a reasonable and fair statement," commented Del, anxiously waiting for an explanation as to why he was calling.

"Well," Trevor continued, "I know you're wondering why I'm calling. I hope I'm not interrupting anything, but it's important."

"Don't worry," Del assured him, "You're not interrupting anything. What's up?"

"It's about Wendy. She's in real danger, and I need to talk to both of you about that. Leo Malone's people are planning to nab her and use her to lure me into a trap. We need to meet and discuss this situation."

"We're anxious to meet with you, Trevor. Just say when and where, and we'll be there."

"Can you put Wendy back on?"

"Sure. Here she is," he handed the phone back to Wendy.

"What's going on, Trev?" she asked.

"Sis, I don't want you to mention any place names over the phone in case your signal's intercepted, but do you remember where we built that fort when we were kids?"

"Yeah, I remember that place."

"Good. I've gone by there twice in the last six months, and it hasn't changed too much. You shouldn't have any problems finding it again. If you and Del could meet me there in two hours…"

"We'll be there."

"Perfect. Oh, and Sis?"

"Yes, Trev, what is it?"

"Be careful. Promise me you'll be careful, and that you'll watch out for anything unusual."

"Like what?"

"Anything. Just be careful."

"I'll be careful," she said with a sigh, "Honestly Trev, you worry too much."

Probably nothing would have surprised Wendy and Del more than Trevor's phone call. Wendy was beginning to seriously wonder whether or not she would ever be able to talk to him again before he called. Del was also growing increasingly frustrated as he was beginning to suspect that he might have already exhausted every possible lead. Certainly the last thing either expected was for him to ring Wendy's cell phone. But after what Trevor just said, Del understood the urgency of the situation. Trevor's worries seemed perfectly warranted to Del, knowing the way Malone did things. He had his .38 Super with him most of the time now in a concealed shoulder holster as part of his normal work clothes, and he realized he may need to rely on it at some point just to protect Wendy, if for no other reason. Malone's people all carried guns, and most of them were as ruthless as any Malone's money could buy.

When they exited Wendy's apartment Del noticed an unmarked car with two men sitting in it parked across the street, about eighty yards away. They could be news media reporters, he realized, but more likely undercover law enforcement. He was almost certain they weren't L.A.P.D. He was pretty familiar with the cars they used. If he had to lay down money on it, he would bet they were F.B.I. The local police weren't especially anxious to see Trevor taken off the streets right now, Del learned from one of his old friends on the force. He was making them look too good.

The other thought he couldn't avoid was that they might be Malone's people. If that were the case, things could be turning rather dangerous sooner than expected. Trevor had warned Wendy to be careful. Del had years of experience with all kinds of different danger, and he knew how to spot trouble. Wendy didn't seem too worried by Trevor's warning. Keeping her out of harm's way was going to be completely up to Del, at least until they met with Trevor and heard what he wanted to tell them.

They managed to lose the car that followed them as soon as they left Wendy's apartment. Del drove his own car, because he knew how to drive so that other drivers would have a difficult time keeping track of him. He'd had to lose following cars before, and he knew that in the line of work he'd chosen for himself now, he'd have to lose other cars again.

The small field where Wendy and Trevor played as kids more than twenty years earlier, along with some weathered remnants of their childhood "fort" still remained, unlike most of the other previously vacant fields in that part of the city that had since been changed by developers. It was less than a half a mile from the house they grew up in. Wendy hadn't been back to the area in years, but just like Trevor predicted, she didn't have any trouble finding it.

Del recognized the van as soon as he saw it, even though now it was a different color. And Wendy recognized her brother almost as soon as she saw him. His disguise was impressive, she had to admit, but she didn't have any trouble recognizing him even with it.

The first thing he asked them was whether or not they suspected anyone had followed them. Del explained that they had been followed initially, but he was certain he'd lost them at least three miles from this place. He also noted that he wasn't sure who the men were. Trevor nodded as if he knew, but he didn't say.

"Trev, why don't you end all of this craziness and return to Luppert Systems?" Wendy asked almost immediately, "The company needs you. They all miss you terribly. We all do. But that's where your talent lies. You're an inventor and an innovator, not a bounty hunter or whatever they call it."

He shook his head, "It's too late for that now. I've stirred up too much. But I didn't want to meet with you here to discuss that. We've got some urgent matters to discuss, and I'm really glad I've got you both here."

"What do you know specifically about Malone's intentions?" asked Del.

"Not much, except that he plans to kidnap Wendy to get to me, like I mentioned earlier. I was able to eavesdrop on a meeting he had with some of his henchmen only a matter of hours ago, and I caught that much. Didn't get a lot of details, but I heard enough to know that Wendy will be in a lot of danger if she stays here. I recommend the two of you take a short vacation out of the state."

"We just came back from a trip to Oregon," she said, "I'm not anxious to go anywhere else for awhile. I'm tired of hotels, quite frankly."

Trevor grew impatient, "Damn it, Sis! I'm asking you to do something to try to save your life. I don't want to be responsible for your safety here in Los Angeles. It's just too risky for you here," he shook his head, "I knew you'd reject my suggestion. You were always that stubborn. That's why I wanted to talk to both of you. Maybe Del can talk some sense into your head. This is your safety I'm talking about here."

"There isn't a single reason why you should feel responsible for my well being. I'm an adult who is fully capable of taking care of herself."

"I'm responsible because I created the problem. Leo Malone is a monster, and he'll use you to get to me. This isn't a game, Sis. This is serious stuff. If Malone got his hands on you, he'd kill you as soon as he got what he wanted. I'm responsible, whether you're willing to admit it, or not. I wish that just for once you'd listen to what I say."

"I agree with your brother," Del chimed with Trevor, "Leo Malone is a powerful man, and he'll spend any amount of money it takes to have whatever he wants done. He's a bad, bad man, Wendy. I could try to protect you here, but…It'd be a lot safer to get out of the city for a week or two—until this whole thing blows over. Plenty of interesting places we could enjoy visiting. You're the photographer. Think of the opportunities."

She looked at Del with surprise, "Mr. Mackenzie, I do believe you're genuinely worried about me. Well, thank you both for your concern, but my life is right here. I don't need to run away from anything. That life wouldn't be worth living."

"I shouldn't have warned you about the danger." Trevor said, frustrated, "I should've just kidnapped you myself and locked you away until I could get Malone put behind bars where he belongs."

Wendy turned to Del, "See what I mean? As far back as I could remember he's wanted to protect me from my own shadow. He'd like to monitor and control every aspect of my life if he only could. Lord knows he's tried. But I'm an adult now, and I'm my own person. I can take care of myself."

Trevor threw up his hands, "I give up. Del, if you can talk some sense into her, you're a better man than I. All I came here to say is that Malone's got some evil tricks up his sleeve, and he didn't get to where he is now by lacking determination. You're a target, Wendy, and that's a dangerous position to be in."

Even if she understood the peril her own life was in, she sure didn't show it. But Trevor expected the reaction from her that he encountered, and Del had gotten to know her well enough to not be surprised by it.

"She's stubbornly independent, your sister is," Del remarked, "but I'm falling for her anyway."

Trevor looked at Wendy, then at Del and nodded. "I know." He said. How could anybody *not* fall for her? Of course he was. Trevor would, too, if she wasn't his sister. Of that he was certain. She was one of a kind, all right. But right now it was comforting to know that she was close to somebody like Del. He was an ex-cop and a competent detective, and he was experienced in dangerous situations. He ought to be able to keep her safe, if anybody could. Besides, he understood the danger she was in. He knew all about Leo Malone.

Even so, Trevor couldn't help worrying. After hearing for himself exactly what Malone was planning, he couldn't help it. Wendy was in real danger, and Trevor knew that as long as Malone was free to conduct his business, he would have professionals working to grab her whenever and wherever they could. If they got her, she could face a terrible end. It was unthinkable. The whole deal couldn't be more disagreeable to Trevor.

If she didn't take this situation more seriously, she probably wouldn't be prepared for the worst, and she would be more likely to fall into whatever traps Malone set out there for her. But there wasn't much Trevor could do about that. That was Wendy.

All that he would be able to do, really, was monitor the situation and keep himself ready to intervene. He could watch Wendy, and to some degree he could watch Malone. Because Del was almost always with Wendy now, Malone's people would no doubt be watching him, too. Trevor knew he could use Del's help with the complexities involved in this kind of surveillance operation, but using his help might not be particularly practical in this situation, the way things were. It was probably much better for Wendy to have Del close to her all the time.

"Thanks for the warning," said Del with genuine gratitude, "Sometimes knowledge is everything. In this case it could mean the difference between life and death for your sister. If we could just find any damning evidence at all on Malone's operations, we could have him put away for a long time. Maybe the two of us could cook up some kind of sting and finally nail him to the wall."

"I've thought about that a lot," Trevor responded, "That would definitely simplify matters. You guys have tried to get him on things before, but you never managed to make anything stick."

Del nodded, "He spends a lot of money on lawyers. He's always hired the best talent in town. Beyond that he's just been lucky."

"Well, maybe his luck is about to run out. Plotting to use my baby sister to get to me could prove hazardous to his condition. If you have any ideas, I'm all ears."

"How do we reach you?"

"You won't have to. I'll keep in contact with you. It's too soon for me to establish any connections. I'm laying low for awhile, where I can operate freely."

"I know about the bugs. Found some in my apartment, and some in Wendy's, too. But I'll leave them be for now. I want to keep a channel open between us. If things start getting crazy, I hope you'll be listening."

Trevor grinned, "I wondered whether you'd found any yet. Guess I could have done a better job hiding them."

"They were hidden pretty well I thought," Del assured him, "I just happened to be looking diligently for some kind of surveillance system, after the little episode at the bridge. Once I finally found one, I started looking extra hard for others. They weren't at all easy to find. But like I said, right now I'm glad they're there. I just hope you'll be listening when things start happening."

"Don't worry, I'll be listening," Trevor said.

After leaving the area, Del learned almost immediately that Wendy was annoyed with him.

"How long have you known about the surveillance bugs?" she asked with an edge.

"I don't know. A couple of weeks, maybe."

"A couple of weeks?" she shrieked, "You've known something like that for a couple weeks and didn't tell me? Did you forget who you're working for?"

"When would I have had a chance to say anything about it without your brother discovering we knew? It's true I found some bugs, but I had no way of knowing how many more he'd hidden, or where he might have hidden any others. You hired me to find Trevor, and I had reason to believe the best way to do that probably was to play along with his game. I sure didn't want to risk severing the only link we had. What would your brother have done if he thought we were on to him?"

She was quiet for a short spell, "Okay," she finally admitted, "you've made your point. But I just don't much care for being kept in the dark on something as important as that. I don't like us keeping secrets from each other. I feel that since you were working for me, you should have kept me informed about anything you discovered involving my brother. That's why I hired you."

"Thought you hired me to *find* your brother. I didn't expect to be able to find him easier by drawing attention to his secret. May not have been the best decision on my part, but that was my logic behind it. Of course, now you've found your brother, which was what you set out to do. Now I can get back to my regular work."

"Got a lot of new clients waiting in line for your services, do you?" she asked with a hint of sarcasm.

"Everyone's got to start somewhere I guess. When I get back to spending some time in the office, I'm bound to get into some new cases soon enough. Maybe nothing quite like this, but there will be cases."

"You need a secretary," she reminded him.

"And you want a job," he reminded her.

"But first, I need to hire a bodyguard. This case isn't over. You heard what he said; my life is in danger."

"So you do believe him after all."

"Maybe. But aren't you at all curious about how much this job will pay?"

"Should I be? We both know you aren't going to let me refuse your job offer, no matter what I say. The fact that I'm not a professional bodyguard is completely irrelevant. You just like being my boss."

"I'm paying five-hundred a day, plus expenses, just like the last job. The only difference is now you have to promise to keep me informed on everything. No more secrets."

"Well, it's a dirty job all right, as the old cliché goes, but somebody's got to do it."

Her mood of irritation had melted away, and now she smiled, "I knew you'd accept. But you have to promise."

"I promise," he said, "no more secrets."

Later that same evening when the two of them left Wendy's apartment seeking a few relaxing hours of entertainment at the cinema as a temporary diversion from the recent craziness, Del suspected at one point that they might have been followed.

He thought he'd seen the same car behind them in the traffic for at least a mile and a half. He wasn't sure that it was the same car, but he didn't want to take any chances.

He took a longer route to the movie-theater and made some unpredictable turns until he was satisfied he'd lost the car.

Even with the extra driving they arrived a full half-hour before the movie started to have the best choices of available seating locations. Del wasn't particularly comfortable with any seats forward of the back wall. He wanted all of the other movie watchers sitting in front of them where no opportunities would exist for surprises. Wendy thought it was an unnecessary precaution, but she didn't argue with him about it. After all, she wanted him to think she'd actually hired him to protect her, even though the larger reason was almost obvious. It provided her with a perfect excuse for keeping him close to her night and day. At least for now, that arrangement was appealing to her.

Just two seconds after choosing their seats, she jumped up to make a fast run to the snack bar for popcorn before the movie started. He wasn't at all comfortable with the idea of letting her out of his sight, at least in a public place like this. But when he realized he couldn't talk her out of it, he simply requested that she hurry back. She assured him that she would, then left the room.

After ten minutes of waiting his anxiety level began to climb, and he considered leaving the chosen seats to venture out into the lobby and find out what was keeping her. But as soon as the thought entered his head, he dismissed it as paranoia. The theater was fast filling up with people and the lines at the snack bar he knew would be long. She would be just lucky if she could get her popcorn and make it back inside of ten minutes.

As the minute hand of his wristwatch approached show time, the seats in the theater were fast filling up. If he got up to go check on her, they'd surely lose their seats along the back wall. But it seemed to be taking her an awfully long time just to buy a bag of popcorn. To Del it seemed unusually long. Maybe it was just his anxiety magnifying everything in his mind.

By the time the ceiling lights were turned off in the theater and the movie previews started, Del was worried. He could think of no good reason why Wendy shouldn't have gotten her popcorn and returned to her seat within the twenty-five minutes she was gone. Unless she had to make an emergency trip to the ladies' room first, it shouldn't have taken that long. The snack bar lines were usually pretty short around the time the movie was supposed to start. She would have had more than enough time to wait in line, make her selection of what she wanted, buy it, and then find her way back to her seat. It wasn't a large enough theater where someone could get lost.

Three minutes after the movie started the crowd had pretty much settled down. Wendy still hadn't returned. Del knew there had to be something else besides popcorn to distract her, and he finally vacated his seat and ventured out of the room to investigate.

He found almost nobody in the lobby, and certainly no long lines at the snack bar. He asked the snack bar attendants if any of them remembered seeing a woman of her description, but none of them did. Of course, that wouldn't be surprising whether she bought her popcorn there or not, because they sell so much popcorn to so many people in such a short amount of time. Individual faces might be hard to remember. Hers apparently was.

He glanced over at the ladies' room. It would be the only other reasonable place for her to be. There was nobody outside the door, and he didn't hesitate to pop his head inside and call for Wendy. He heard no answer, so he called her name again and still heard no answer.

"Is anyone in here?" he then yelled, again hearing the sound of his voice echoing off the tile floors and walls. Nobody answered, so he stepped inside and checked each stall. He found the facility completely empty. Just to be thorough, he checked the men's rest room as well, now with his gun drawn. Again his searching turned up nothing.

At this point he knew that something was definitely very wrong. She wouldn't do something like this on her own knowing his concerns about her safety, particularly after their meeting with Trevor earlier. She didn't lack a sense of humor, but this just wasn't her kind of joke. Del knew her well enough to know that. It wouldn't be like her to test him this way.

He could be sure that she didn't make her way back into the theater while he was stepping out because she would have had to pass him in the hallway to get back in from the lobby. But he didn't want to leave any stone unturned, so he went back in to check the line of seats against the back wall. Just as he expected, she hadn't returned to her seat, and the seats in the back row were now all filled by latecomers.

Suddenly he was faced with the very crisis he was depended upon to prevent, and for the first time in a long time, he was at a complete loss as to what his next move should be. He had to presume that Wendy had been kidnapped by Malone's people just as Trevor had warned them about. But he hadn't expected any attempts to be made this soon. And he suddenly found himself without a plan of action.

As an ex-police officer, his initial inclination was to call one or two of his old friends and explain the entire situation. It certainly warranted a thorough police investigation. Under the present circumstances, he knew they would start an official criminal investigation immediately, based only on what he had to tell them. And he couldn't deny his obligation to report something like this.

But something about that bothered him. Maybe it was the awareness that Malone always managed to make evidence completely disappear whenever he suspected the police were looking into anything he was involved in. And somehow, Malone always managed to know when the police were getting close. He either had one of his own people in the Department—a rat nobody ever suspected, or he had some kind of special extrasensory perception. Whatever it was, it made that option; going to the police, too risky as far as Del was concerned.

He'd have to find another strategy for exposing Leo Malone. The police had failed in that regard consistently. Wendy's life was too precious to Del to leave it in the hands of the Department. There would have to be another option.

But Del wasn't sure just where he would begin his search for her. His mind was buzzing with troubling thoughts as he left the theater, struggling trying to assemble some sort of plan. He knew where Malone lived, and he knew where Malone's office, or more accurately, his headquarters, was located. It was potentially useful knowledge, but he knew that Wendy wouldn't be held at either of those places, and wherever she was, she wasn't going to be saved by any uninvited visits to those locations. Malone had too many hired guns. Del knew he'd have to come up with a better plan.

After leaving the theater, he drove directly to her apartment and waited there for a while. By this time he had his own key. But it was exactly as he expected, and she never came home. Pretty soon he realized that he had never felt so alone in his entire life. The bright light that had recently seemed to appear from nowhere into his world had suddenly vanished without much warning, and it became more and more difficult for him to think about with every passing hour.

He reminded himself that the purpose of her abduction, according to Trevor, was to bring her brother out of hiding for a confrontation. It was Trevor they were after. Wendy was merely the trap's bait. And they wouldn't be concerning themselves too much with Del, if they even knew he existed. That should give him a slight advantage in this ugly business.

He thought about how much easier a case is to work on when one isn't emotionally involved. He never really had that particular dilemma before, but he sure had it now. And he was mindful that if he wasn't careful, his emotions could interfere with his clear thinking. Now wasn't the time for that. There was just too much at stake.

He started wondering how long it would be before the word got out about her disappearance. Ever since her relationship to the Vigilante had been made known publicly, there was a lot of attention focused on her. How long would it take someone to figure out that she was now missing as well? Del hoped they wouldn't figure it out too soon. If news broke about that, it sure wouldn't make her easier to find. It would have the undesired effect of forcing her captors to be more careful, and hide her away better than they might otherwise. In the very least, it would complicate everything. Del knew he probably didn't have much time before that would happen, if he didn't come up with a workable plan first. That's what he needed to concentrate on right now; coming up with a workable plan.

It was almost eleven o'clock that night when he finally returned to his own apartment, by then feeling ready to collapse onto his bed and close his tired eyes. It had been a long exhausting day.

But his head wouldn't be hitting the pillow quite as soon as he had hoped. As he turned onto the street of his apartment, he noticed the van parked in front. The image of Trevor's unusual van on the street in front of his apartment filled him with mixed feelings. There was a sense of dread with the thought of explaining to him that his sister was missing, maybe an ounce of resentment over the whole sequence of events resulting from Trevor's activities, and probably more than anything, he felt a sense of relief that he wouldn't be alone in his search now. Two minds were almost always better than one.

He pulled his car into his space under the carport, parked it, and then stepped out to walk over to the parked van. He took a deep breath and prepared his explanation about what had occurred earlier.

CHAPTER X

Trevor didn't appear to be at all surprised, and even more amazingly, he didn't seem especially worried. Del's sense was that Wendy's brother had a plan in his head of some sort, which was more than he had at this stage of the game. And any tendency either may have had to want to blame the other for what had happened was completely overshadowed by the obvious need for them to work together as a team.

Del was an experienced detective who had proven his worth as a law enforcement officer, and Trevor had the resources and technology to make almost any seemingly impossible mission possible. They would make an effective team as long as they worked closely together, and each had that expectation. They had the same objective in mind; finding Wendy and freeing her from the danger she was facing.

Their first order of business, they both agreed, was to establish some level of surveillance on Malone and his employees. Because this would be the expected strategy, they'd have to be especially clever. Malone was surely waiting for it, and that would make it a whole lot riskier than if he wasn't.

What they really needed was someone on the inside of Malone's organization who could keep them informed on current events concerning Wendy. But setting up something along those lines would be a trick, all right. It was worth talking about perhaps, regardless of how unachievable it might seem. It would have to be something creative, something as unexpected as that to successfully circumvent Malone's security.

There would have to be some observation before any plan of that sort would develop. They would have to watch Malone's people, and decide which one of them, if any, would serve their purpose.

"I expected this van to be loaded with sophisticated gear," Del explained, looking around inside the vehicle upon Trevor's invitation, "but this is even more amazing than I imagined."

"Remember this thing?" Trevor asked, drawing Del's attention to the thermal viewing device.

Del looked surprised, "Yes, I do as a matter of fact. But I was told that although it is your own invention, a working model wasn't actually manufactured until *after* you disappeared."

"You were told right," answered Trevor, "and in fact, I'm pretty sure that this is the exact same unit you field tested. I think they've made only one prototype. I'm just borrowing it for awhile."

"And your verdict?"

"They got it mostly right. Needs more testing. But for what we need it for I think it'll serve."

Again Del looked around inside the van, obviously impressed by everything he saw, "Must be a heck of a lot to keep track of," he said.

"It can be, especially for just one guy. But the capabilities it provides me with make it all worth it. Let me show you what some of this stuff does."

He proceeded to explain some of the equipment in the van and how to use it. There were monitors and control modules crowding the van's inside walls, along with cables, switches, LED lights, and other odd electronic components.

"Must take an awful lot of power to keep all of this stuff operating," Del commented.

"I've got enough battery juice to keep a shopping mall lit up for two days, with maybe a little left over. You wouldn't believe the size of the auxiliary battery this van has."

"For some reason I believe I actually would," Del said. After seeing all of this elaborate equipment, there wasn't much else that would surprise him.

Trevor explained how he was able to do certain things, such as intercept cell phone communications, tap into land lines the old fashioned way, decode passwords and gain access to systems, etc.

"A lot of this could be especially useful in your line of work," Trevor noted.

Del nodded in agreement. He knew he could learn a lot from Trevor, and especially now he was particularly eager to learn. Trevor had his full attention.

Before the sun was completely over the metropolitan horizon the following morning, they set about preparing their trap for one of Malone's employees. They knew where to find them.

They debated awhile about whether or not to attempt to go directly after the boss himself, and apply all of the persuasive measures their imaginations could conceive to get him to reveal Wendy's whereabouts. But they finally agreed that that plan was probably the least practical. His security had too many layers. And he would be expecting that kind of reaction from Trevor—it was the whole purpose of Wendys kidnapping. He'd be prepared for it. That particular strategy would be playing right into Malone's goals. Besides, he was known to be as stubborn as an ox. There would be no guarantee that any measure of coercion would make him talk. Trevor and Del were both mindful how sensitive the situation was. Whatever plan they went with, if it backfired, it could end really badly for Wendy and they couldn't ignore the worst-case scenario, no matter how hard either of them tried.

The building occupied by Malone's office was wired with several different security systems. Trevor was knowledgeable about these, and he had circumvented them successfully before. He knew that he could get back into the office with the right timing, and with the right assistance. Del would be useful here. He'd been in enough precarious situations throughout his career to know how to handle them. Trevor was confident that Del would be able to keep a cool head, and that's what was needed here. With a careful plan that accounted for every detail, they could get into Malone's office undetected, and spin their new monitoring web. There would be no room for even the slightest mistake. Precision was the key. But Trevor and Del were both motivated to prove that it was achievable.

By five-thirty a.m. they were in the office, masked and wearing rubber gloves, moving cautiously as if stepping through an obstacle course. Trevor understood the security systems, and he was familiar with Malone's office, so Del gladly followed his lead. Del was thoroughly impressed by Trevor's mastery of the whole operation, and he said so in a low whisper Trevor could hardly hear.

"What was that you said?" Trevor asked him.

"Nothing. Just glad you're not on their side, that's all."

"Well, this might not have worked without both of us. It would have been a lot tougher alone, anyway. A lot riskier."

Trevor had his black gadget bag with him, full of specialty tools and surveillance gear. He proceeded to prepare a tiny fiber-optic video camera for mounting inside the wall while Del carefully pried a section of the thin molding loose around the window frame. They cut out a small cavity in the sheet rock behind the molding just large enough to house the camera, and with a cordless drill a pinhole was drilled through the strip of molding at that spot to allow the camera to view most of the area within the office. The camera was equipped with a very small transmitter, operating off of a pill-sized lithium battery that had a power life span of forty-eight hours. That was expected to be more time than they would need.

With some creative fitting, Del was able to restore the molding to where it would be next to impossible for anyone to notice without close scrutiny. Trevor found several other ideal locations to hide microphones, and he planted a total of three. If one or two were discovered, they could still listen to the people in the room.

Once they'd done what they came to do, they made their way back out of the building slowly, confident that they hadn't tripped any silent alarms or left behind any trace of their visit. It was already past six o'clock and the street was partially illuminated by the newly appearing sun. The streetlights had already turned off. The nighttime doorman, who was also on Malone's payroll, was never aware that anyone had entered the building before business hours. Del and Trevor had gone in and out through an air conditioning vent on the back wall. They managed to get in quietly, and were confident that nobody saw them enter or exit.

Now it was just a matter of waiting until people started showing up for work, and then closely monitoring them in order to decide who would be the best choice to grab, and the best way to snare him. This was a good idea. The only other scenario that could possibly be better would be if they heard somebody say the exact location where they were holding Wendy. If they got so lucky, they wouldn't need to bother trying to grab one of them. But that would be a long shot. Especially now, Malone made sure his people were careful about what they said, just about everywhere. He could be awfully careful that way, even in his own office a lot of the time when he perceived the need to be. His people would learn how to speak a lot in coded phrases, just in case somebody was listening.

It was part of the reason the police were having such a hard time getting something useful out of watching him for such a long time. He may have been a loose cannon in some ways, but when he suspected he was under surveillance, it was usually difficult for a spy to nail him to the wall. He hadn't survived this long entirely by luck.

Del and Trevor were now able to do what they needed to do, which was to observe and learn. When they could establish for certain who drove what car, they could track those cars. When they were able to positively match faces to voices, they could keep track of them easily. It wouldn't take long to know everything they needed to know about everyone who worked for Leo Malone.

There would be roughly an hour of waiting before people would start showing up for work. Del and Trevor were used to this kind of waiting. Experience had taught both of them patience. They waited in Trevor's van, ready with the surveillance equipment on.

"You and Wendy seem to hit it off pretty well," Trevor said, refining the imaging on his monitor, "She's hired you to find me?"

"That was the initial arrangement," Del said.

"And now that I'm found?"

"Now that the two of you have had a chance to talk, no thanks to my efforts, that particular job is over."

"But you are still working for?"

"Ha!" Del blurted, "She hired me back on, just before she disappeared, as her *bodyguard*. How am I doing so far?" he sarcastically asked.

Trevor looked at Del with a serious look.

"Don't blame yourself for her disappearance, Delmar. You weren't the one who got her into this in the first place. But then, before you go on blaming me, as justifiable as that might be, understand this: We're going to find out where she is, and we're going to save her from harm. I've made my share of mistakes lately, I know. But I promise you that. I've been watching a lot, and I know you've got feelings for her. I know. We will get Wendy out of this."

Del sighed, "I know we will. Still can't help the worrying."

"Neither can I, my friend, but we'll find Wendy. We've *got* to. She's my only sister."

The view of the office through the pinhole in the window frame molding was from behind Malone's desk, which provided a clear picture of everyone in the room besides Malone, who had his back to the camera most of the time. Trevor and Del were able to record images of faces, and hear the sounds of their voices. They would be able to easily recognize each man, and noting the vehicle each arrived in, would be able to attach tracking devices to the appropriate cars. By the time the first meeting of the day was concluded, they were able to identify four of Malone's people by either face or voice, and had recorded the plate numbers on each one's car, as well as getting a tracking device on each car.

"My system can track up to half a dozen vehicles simultaneously," Trevor explained, "as long as they all stay within a fifty mile radius."

They both realized there was a pretty good possibility that one of these employees could lead them directly to where Wendy was being held before they would have to kidnap anybody. That would be the easiest scenario, if not necessarily the best. It would mean fewer risky confrontations, but also probably less information.

Of the four employees in the office, two were ruled out fairly early. Their loyalty to their boss appeared surprisingly strong. Maybe they had worked for Malone a long time, or maybe they were just naïve. It could also have been just an act to win their boss's favor, but that would be too risky to bet on. Those two also appeared to be in top physical condition. One had a street hardened face, and the other seemed unusually perceptive. Either of them could be especially difficult to manage, it was decided.

Of the other two, one appeared to be more careless than the other in his actions and mannerisms. He might be the easiest to catch off guard. But he gave no indication that he knew where Wendy was, or whether he even knew about her abduction. They observed him closely hoping to pick up any clues about what he knew. Malone's people were all a bit more careful about what they said now. There was a certain atmosphere of caution, as if there was almost a presumption they were being monitored.

They continued to focus their attention on him. The others in the office called him Robby. Del and Trevor would watch him until they saw an opportunity to grab him quietly, and they hoped he would serve the purpose they needed him for.

Already they knew his voice, his face, his first name, what kind of car he drove, and his license plate number. They decided to stalk him and learn more. Before the end of the day they would know where he lived, who he lived with if anyone, and quite a bit more of his story. This was an information business above all else.

Nothing was said about it aloud, but each could sense that the other enjoyed this kind of activity. Spying on people provided a certain intrigue unlike any other occupation. And it was addicting enough to keep them both awake through a night whenever there was activity to monitor. Night operations had become one of Trevor's specialties, and Del was learning some new things from him in that area.

They followed Robby's car to an apartment complex in another part of the city, where he parked it. They watched him exit his car and enter the building, and they wasted no time getting to their task.

There was no way to know how much time they would have, but their operation was efficient. Del kept a close surveillance on the apartment building while Trevor got into Robby's car and planted the microphones and transmitter. They could communicate with each other via the voice-activated close range radio headsets each wore.

Del noticed that Trevor was waving some sort of odd instrument over Robby's car before proceeding to break in. It looked something like a hair dryer.

"What is that?" Del asked in a whisper.

"It's an alarm deactivator." Trevor responded, speaking into the microphone of his headset as he worked, "It works on the principle of electromagnetism. It disables any alarms that might be set off when the vehicle is entered without a key. You never know about these newer vehicles. The task is pretty risky without this device."

"It's a darn good thing car thieves don't have that technology," commented Del.

"Unfortunately they're starting to figure some of these things out for themselves. Eventually they'll be able to defeat any car alarm currently on the market. That's what's so scary about it. There is really no way to stop that from happening. Hey, I sure hope you're keeping your eyes on that apartment."

"Don't worry. Hardly took my eyes off it for even a fraction of a second. Your field is clear. How much longer do you expect it to take?"

"Almost done."

"That's a relief. I was beginning to wonder if you were attempting to re-upholster the car's whole interior."

"Just trying to make sure he won't find what I'm putting into his car. Hey, are you getting nervous already?"

"I think I'm well past that point," answered Del.

"Good, because after he leaves his apartment, we're going to bug that, too."

"Just like Malone's office."

"All but the camera."

A minute later Trevor returned to his van, having accomplished everything he needed to accomplish at Robby's car.

"There's one mission accomplished," he said, "Now we'll be able to listen to him in his car, and trace his travels on our screen. We'll be able to watch his car wherever he goes."

Del shook his head, "Some of the surveillance technology you've developed is almost too good to be true."

"Actually," Trevor admitted with genuine modesty, "a lot of it has existed for awhile. Surely you're familiar with some of this stuff, or at least variations of these things. I'd be surprised if L.A.P.D. didn't have similar tools in its toolbox. Am I right?"

Del tried to think specifically.

"We had some nice products to work with sometimes, but the Department was always budget conscious. It's usually the federal agencies that get the best toys. I think most police departments are often reluctant to authorize the use of anything new or untested in the courts. Been awhile since I've worked undercover assignments. I remember renting whatever we needed from the local security specialists."

"Most everyone in the security business in Southern California these days buys their products from Lupert Systems," Trevor noted proudly.

"Then you invented most of what everyone is using," Del surmised.

"Not necessarily invented. Improved upon, to be sure. In the field of special operations, most of my products have been employed in one variation or another for quite awhile before I ever got into the business. What I've managed to do again and again was to refine existing technology. I've studied these devices for years and tried to figure out how to make them better—more practical, and usually more efficient. I was pretty successful with that."

"Would you ever want to go back to Luppert Systems? I mean, if you could?"

Trevor paused, thinking about what it would be like to go back, doing what he was so good at.

"I've thought about it a few times since all of this. I enjoyed going to work, experimenting with circuits and new technologies. I guess if I were still there, doing what I had been doing, I'd have no complaints about it. It was fun for me. But of course, that's not possible now. I've got no regrets, as far as my career goes. And what about you? You've made quite a career change yourself?"

"I don't know yet. I think it's too early for me to decide whether or not I made a good choice," Del answered. The subject made him think of how he became better acquainted with Wendy.

They kept a close watch on Robby over the next day and a half, hoping to learn about Wendy's whereabouts without having to disrupt his routine. They were mindful that his coming up missing could take some of the surprise out of their activities when his boss learned of it. It would sure be ideal to be able to avoid all of that, but they weren't getting anywhere presently. They had no clues yet. It was time to start planning their strategy, now that they knew as much as they knew about his daily routine, and they knew what they had to do.

Robby Florentine had been hired by Leo Malone primarily because he knew the people in the Los Angeles narcotics business. He'd been dealing drugs for years without ever getting himself arrested. He had contacts on the streets, and he could move "product". Of course, the fact that he had Italian blood running through his veins didn't hurt anything, as far as his position in Malone's organization was concerned.

But he wasn't really a tough guy. He obviously wasn't one of Malone's hired guns. But Malone's organization was a tight group, and it was reasonable to expect he knew something about Wendy's abduction. If he did happen to know where Wendy was, he would be the perfect subject for interrogation, Trevor and Del were both thinking. After watching him for nearly two days, they concluded that he should be an egg easily cracked under the right kind of pressure.

The van followed Robby's new Camaro all the way to Long Beach. Del and Trevor quickly learned what the trip was about, because Robby couldn't stay off of his cell phone. He was picking up a cash deposit and delivering a small shipment of cocaine to one of Malone's new business associates. Del recognized some of the lingo used in the trade, and was able to fill in the blanks. That was from his past experiences working in the narcotics division. Most people wouldn't have known exactly what he was talking about from the kind of words he was using. Trevor considered himself to be a pretty decent code breaker, but listening to Robby on his cell phone challenged his skills. Del was occasionally grateful for his own career background. It helped in things like this.

They waited until after he concluded his business behind the crowded snack bar, and after the buyer left with the two gym bags full of drugs and Robby had the cash-filled briefcase in his possession, Trevor casually approached him and flashed a badge. He spoke quickly, implying that he had the whole deal on tape. He nodded in the direction of Del, who stood across the crowd watching everything with a walkie-talkie at his ear, as if he was communicating with the "rest of the team".

"Oh, you could try to run, Mr. Florentine," Trevor said casually, "but we've got the whole deal recorded, and this time we secured a warrant in advance, so that it'll all hold up in court. And we know where you live. We know all your friends. If you want to make a run for it, now's your chance. Four of us are betting on how far you'll get. But it's not you we're after. Work with us, and you just might stay out of jail. We're after the big boss."

"Who did you say you were again?" he looked at Trevor suspiciously.

"Federal Bureau of Investigation, Mr. Florentine. I showed you my identification. I'm Officer Warren, and my partner over there is Officer Daniels. You'll be getting to know a few of us over the next couple of weeks, whether or not you had other plans. But we've got most of what we want on Leo Malone already. He'll be behind bars before Christmas, my friend, make no mistake about that. We're getting our case together quite nicely. The question you want to ask yourself right now is whether or not you want to spend the next twenty-five to fifty years of your life behind bars, along with your boss, or would you be interested in making a deal? It's as simple as that, and it doesn't make much difference to us either way. This is the best shot you're going to get. We have most of what we need, but we could use your help in finishing this, if that's the route you want to go."

Robby sat down on the closest bench seat, and started thinking real hard. His face showed a bewildered look. Trevor could see the tiny beads of sweat forming on his forehead, and he gently reached for the briefcase. Robby offered no resistance, and Trevor took the briefcase as naturally as if he was conducting routine business.

"We'll need this for evidence," he said.

"How do I know you're not bluffing just to get me to incriminate my boss?" Robby questioned, as would be expected with someone in his shoes, "Maybe it's a trick. Maybe you don't really have anything right now worth its weight, and you're fishing for what you need."

"Oh, we have quite a lot of evidence, all right. We have enough to put him away for three lifetimes. We're looking at more than just sending him to prison. Someone's life happens to be in jeopardy at the moment, a completely innocent person, and we're hoping to keep that person out of harm's way, if that's possible. But it is true that you haven't seen the mountain of evidence we've been collecting for months. If you'd be so kind as to join us back to one of the FBI offices, we'll show you some of what we do have now. I'm sure you'll find it quite fascinating."

"How can you assure me that I will never see the inside of a prison? That would be the only way I'd ever help anyone against Leo Malone. He can be a dangerous man to doublecross."

"You're familiar with the government's secret witness protection program, aren't you, Mr. Florentine?"

"I've heard of it."

"Well, we're strong believers in the principle that anyone who is willing to take risks helping the FBI should never do hard time. It just wouldn't be right. So, that's our offer. We've got the resources and political influence to keep just about anyone out of jail, if it serves our purpose."

"Maybe I can help you then. *Maybe*. But if I don't deliver that briefcase to my boss in a timely manner, he'll get awfully suspicious, awfully fast. I've worked for him long enough to know."

"We're very much aware of that. But don't worry about it. We're going to replace these bills with special government marked bills, for him. We are required to hold the originals for evidence. Mr. Malone will never know it."

"How long will you detain me at your office?"

"Try not to think of it as being detained. Think of it as a business meeting—a friendly business meeting."

Before reaching the van, Robby was blindfolded, to which he had no objection when it was explained as a routine but necessary procedure, and then he was drugged without any warning to render him unconscious for two hours. That was all the time they needed to set things up.

A room in Del's apartment was hastily converted to an interrogation room, complete with sound proofing panels and a covering over the window. By the time Robby regained consciousness, he found himself strapped to a hospital bed on his back and an unpleasantly bright lamp was shining in his eyes. The rest of the room was dark. Trevor and Del were vague silhouettes in the outer edge of the lamp's light field, and Robby's face revealed his dread of what might happen next.

"Is this considered a usual 'friendly' FBI meeting?" he asked with suspicion.

"Standard interrogation procedures," answered Del, "We're authorized to take this as far as needed to extract the information we seek. The process is always one hundred percent successful, because it doesn't end until the desired information is obtained, and that always happens…eventually. How long it goes on is entirely up to you."

"Oh, jeez!" Robby shrieked, "This *can't* be legal," he tried to lift his head to inspect the nylon webbing holding him down, but he couldn't see them well, "I don't know why we need all this. I told you I'd help you. What exactly do you want to know, anyway?"

"Do you know the name, Wendy Luppert?" Trevor asked him dryly.

There was a pause with silence, then Robby tried to turn his head away from the bright light.

"I think so. What about her?"

"Where is she? Where is your boss holding her?"

"Wait a minute. You guys might not even be with the FBI, like you said. Maybe you work for that Vigilante."

"Does it make any difference to you now who we are? Seems to us that we have the upper hand at the moment. We've got Malone's briefcase full of money, and one of his employees. Not too much you can do about that right now, is there?"

"Look, even if I knew where they were holding her, if I told you I'd be a dead man for sure. You don't know Leo Malone."

"Actually, we do know Leo Malone," Trevor said, "and if you give us the right information, we won't send him a copy of the taped conversation we had earlier when you were ready to sell him out."

"I wasn't going to sell him out!" Robby shouted defensively.

"We know that, and you know that, but what's Mr. Malone going to think when he hears the tape? Would you like for us to play some of it back for you? It sounded as if you were ready to make a deal with us, and send your boss away for a long, long time. I wonder how he would react to that. And then there's the minor detail about the money he trusted you to secure for him. How will you explain about his money coming up missing?"

"What if I don't know where she is? I wasn't involved in picking her up, or arranging any of that whole deal. Malone gives me other jobs. Never that kind of stuff."

"Even if you don't know where she is, you can sure find out easily enough, without tipping them off. We might need to use certain drugs to get the truth out of you, but we were planning on that, anyway. One way or another, we're going to find Wendy, and free her from that bastard you work for. One way or another," Del said, with a cutting edge to his words.

"Who is she to you guys, anyway?"

"She's a lady. She's a *real* lady, and an innocent person. You, your boss, and everyone who works for your boss will be going to hell if anything bad happens to her. We're going to see to that, and that's a promise," Del said.

"Amen!" added Trevor.

CHAPTER XI

Wendy knew they planned on killing her when they were done with her. This was the worst-case scenario that Trevor had warned her about, and it was what Del had been so worried about. She hadn't taken any of it very seriously…until now. Now that it was too late to prevent. Now she could feel the danger she was in, and even worse, she felt a sense of guilt for the danger this was intended to bring to her brother, and that might also endanger Del as well. She hadn't listened very well to their warnings, but now she was sure wishing she had.

They kept her tied up, and a blindfold had been covering her eyes constantly since she'd been here. She never had a very good opportunity to see any of their faces. And she didn't know where she was. From the sounds she could hear from time to time she guessed she was in an old farmhouse somewhere out in the country. This was at least an hour's drive from the heart of Los Angeles, but she wasn't able to estimate which direction the road traveled to reach this place. Her vision had been restricted the instant she was abducted.

She tried to think of some way to escape, but no ideas that seemed practical came to her. Being tied up and not able to see anything around her gave her the most helpless feeling she ever had as far as she could remember. They had someone watching her constantly, and she wasn't even allowed to use the bathroom without an escort. She was conscious of the fact that, even if she managed to get her wrists and ankles free of those heavy plastic lock-ties, which she couldn't imagine being possible without a good serrated knife or heavy snips and probably some help from someone else, none of which were currently available to her, she would still have to use those without drawing her guard's attention. That would be a trick, all right.

They had her gagged for most of the time they held her captive to keep her quiet. The gag was removed only when they let her eat and drink some water, which was only twice each day. She was told she would be shot immediately if she yelled out, but she suspected that was probably a bluff. They obviously had a particular time in mind for killing her, or they would have killed her already. Besides, she never heard any motor vehicle traffic or talking neighbors. The only sounds she could hear through an open window were the jingling of wind chimes apparently hanging under the eves near the porch. This was obviously a quiet country house well secluded, and if she cried for help, it was pretty unlikely that anyone would hear it besides whoever was guarding her. And the guard would surely be annoyed by it at the very least.

She would need to come up with something more practical and less predictable. There was really no way to know how much time she would have before Malone gave the order to end her life. The thought made her shutter. She knew she was currently being kept alive as bait to trap Trevor, and her time remaining depended directly on how long it would take to lure him in. Leo Malone had some kind of special plan in mind, but Wendy knew her brother. He was intelligent and very clever. He would have a plan of his own. Even so, there was an awful lot here that could go wrong. It was impossible for her not to worry.

The tough plastic strips bit into her skin and had been cutting off circulation to some of her fingers and toes. The numbness was almost unbearably uncomfortable. She tried to block it from her mind, though, knowing that it wasn't doing her any good to concentrate on it.

She clung to the tiniest shred of hope that either Del or Trevor would arrive soon with a good plan to get her out of this nightmarish predicament. She knew they'd be working on it, but it had already been three days, and those plastic ties were getting beyond painful. In all likelihood, they wouldn't even know where she was being held. By the time they figured it out, *if* they ever figured it out, it would probably be too late. This ordeal couldn't go on forever.

Wendy's independent nature kept her searching her own mind for ideas about taking action. Ultimately, she realized, her fate was really in her own hands if there was any way out of this. She would either figure something out, or she wouldn't. And she kept reminding herself that no matter how risky any escape effort could be, simply laying back and waiting to be killed would be certain doom.

Getting those plastic ties off of her would require some help. Her guard could be useful in that respect. The fact that he was a man and she was a woman made her ask herself the obvious question: Could he be persuaded to remove them for her if he thought he might have a little fun with her? She'd need to convince him that he would. She was somewhat surprised that he hadn't tried something already, given her vulnerable position. Surely he wasn't above taking advantage of her in her situation. After all, he'd have to know that Malone's intention was to have her killed after she served his purpose. He'd be a complete fool if he didn't understand that.

She hadn't been able to get a good look at the guard. She could hear the sound of his voice, so she knew he was a man, but she wore a blindfold constantly. She tried to imagine what he looked like, but she had no way of knowing. It didn't matter, anyhow.

Communicating could be a problem. Currently she had a folded strip of cloth tightly wrapped around her head holding the rag in place that was stuffed into her mouth to keep her silent. It was now soggy from saliva, but it kept her from yelling out, or even just talking. She could make muffled noises, but she couldn't clearly explain anything to the guard.

After awhile he got tired of listening to her moaning; he knew she was trying to get his attention, so he removed the gag to find out what it was all about.

"Okay, lady, what is your problem?" he asked her, "You powdered your nose just about a half hour ago. If you gotta go now, you'll have to hold it for a while. And if you have an itch, I'm not scratching it. You'll just have to wait it out."

"My blindfold hurts my eyes," she complained.

"That's too bad. You have to keep it on anyway. Boss's rules, not mine."

"I'm dying to know what you look like," she said, "I don't see how me getting a tiny look at you can hurt anything. It's not like I'm trying to get you into any trouble with your boss, or anything like that. I just need to look at a man—a real man," she hoped to plant the seeds of seduction while she still had a chance. She understood the risks, and how it could easily get out of control. But she also saw it as her only chance to change her situation.

"You're a real man, aren't you?" she kept going with it, "I mean, think about it. Here you are, in a house alone with a desperate nymphomaniac, and just think about how much fun we could have. Free up my hands and feet, let me take my clothes off, let me take your clothes off, and let me show you some of what we might do. I can teach you some special things. Let me take a look at you. Your boss doesn't have to know."

155

She listened for his response, but he didn't respond right away. The room was quiet. She knew he was thinking. The thought had to be appealing to him if he was anything like every other man she's ever known. She was an attractive lady and she knew it. Even if he correctly suspected she had some kind of trick in mind, the idea she'd planted in his mind had to be arousing some excitement within him. When his animal instinct would begin to replace his human logic and reasoning, and when his clothes were coming off and his thoughts occupied, she might then have a chance to get away. There maybe a slim chance, but certainly a lot better chance than she had right now. It would probably be the only chance she'd get to have those ties removed.

She tried to listen, but she couldn't tell what he was doing, if anything. He wasn't talking, so he must have been considering what she'd said. He must have been considering it real hard. She noticed that he wasn't quick to gag her back up right away after hearing her erotic ideas. He must have liked what he heard.

Not being able to see anything around her made her feel especially insecure suddenly. She strained to listen to every little sound. And then when she heard what sounded like a belt buckle being unbuckled followed by the sound of a zipper, she started to really worry. He was obviously getting himself undressed, but he hadn't yet freed her hands, or even removed her blindfold, and she detected nothing to suggest that he ever intended to. She realized she'd created a dangerous situation over which she had no control, and it would be next to impossible to undo.

As she listened, she could hear him continuing to remove his clothes, slowly, but he said nothing. She knew what to expect, but she optimistically hoped he wasn't going to be too rough with her. It was hard to imagine anything good that could possibly come of this, the way things were going.

Just then the sound of a vehicle traveling toward the house obviously got his attention, and he stopped undressing. She could tell by the sound of the silence. Then almost immediately he began getting himself dressed as fast as he could to meet whoever was coming up the driveway. It sounded to Wendy like a long gravel driveway. She could hear the guard dressing himself hastily, as if he was nervous about being caught with his pants down.

She continued to listen attentively. She heard the sound of car doors opening and shutting, and men talking outside. The guard frantically getting himself dressed. She had no idea what to expect next.

Then, from what she could gather, the guard met the others at the front door, and it became apparent that Leo Malone was among them. She had never heard his voice before, but there was little doubt as to who was the big boss whenever he entered a room. And she could smell the cigar smoke right away.

"The girl needs to be moved to another location," he stated frankly, after stepping into the house with several of his henchmen. "Mr. Florentine seems to have vanished, and we don't need to be taking any unnecessary chances right now. Hey, why isn't she gagged? I remember giving specific instructions about that."

"I only removed it for five minutes, boss," the guard replied nervously, "Thought she was going to choke on it. Well, uh, keeping her alive was also part of your instructions, too, boss. But I'll gag her back up now that she seems to be okay."

"We may not need to keep her alive too much longer," Malone explained, "I'm guessing that boyfriend of hers, that ex-cop, Mackenzie, knows where to find her brother. If anybody knows, he should. He's a detective, for Christ's sake. Should've considered that sooner. We will find out just how much he knows."

"Del hasn't been able to find Trevor," Wendy blurted out, hoping to keep him out of their focus, if that might be at all possible, "He's been pulling his hair out trying to find him, but it's all been for nothing. He's clueless."

"Who asked you anything?" Malone spoke to her sharply, obviously annoyed by what she said, "Maybe we ought to mail him a couple of your pretty fingers and see how fast he tells us where to find him."

She was horrified by such talk, but she tried not to let it show. She didn't want Malone to have the satisfaction of knowing he was filling her with terror.

"That wouldn't do much good if he doesn't know," she said.

"Shut up!" he ordered her, losing his temper at being contradicted. Then to the guard, "Were you going to gag her in the near future, or will I have to do that myself, too?"

"I'm on it, boss," the guard said, quickly readying the saliva-soaked rag.

Wendy found herself praying for some kind of miracle, realizing that it would take one to get her out of this fix. She was miserably uncomfortable, and she couldn't imagine how she could realistically hope to avoid a tragic end. She estimated there were at least four men in the house, and possibly five. They were going to move her to another location, which she knew meant that she would be spending an hour or two in the hot stuffy trunk of a car, the same way she had been transported to this location. She couldn't avoid her feeling of dread. Even if Del and Trevor both knew where she was being held, they would be outnumbered. And pretty soon she would be at a different place, anyway. She was completely doomed and she knew it. And then things started happening fast.

"Oh, crap!" someone yelled, and the guard dropped the rag he'd been trying to fold back into a gag. It fell onto the side of her neck. Everyone seemed to be scrambling about the house, probably toward the windows to get a better view of the property.

"Well, damn it, what did you see?" demanded Malone.

"Just a glimpse through the curtain of someone darting across the driveway. I swear it looked like someone in uniform, like a SWAT uniform. He took cover behind the limo."

"Anyone else see anything?" Malone asked.

"Can't see a goddamn thing from where I'm at," one of them grumbled.

"Then move your coward ass to a better position," responded another.

Wendy could hear pistols sliding out of holsters and the clicking of safeties being disengaged. Malone's men expected a fight. This was exciting by any measure. Wendy couldn't see what was going on, but she could hear everything. And she could feel the adrenaline.

"How would anyone know about this place?"

"Florentine," said Malone, "He had to have gone to the police. I never really trusted the rat. His big mistake if he's double-crossed me. I'll make him regret it."

"How do we get out of this mess, boss? There's probably a whole bunch of cops out there surrounding this house, looking for a way in. And they're the tactical kind. What do you figure our chances are if we try to shoot our way out?"

"That's what I hired you boys for. That's your department."

"We don't know what we're up against. I can't see anybody. It seems pretty quiet out there right now, anyway."

"Maybe Rick just imagined he saw something."

"Imagined my ass! Okay, Michael, if you think I'm just hallucinating, let's see you go out there and show us that nobody's there. My money says you won't do it."

"Then what are they waiting for? If the cops are here to rescue the lady, how do they know we're not about to cut her throat? What's holding them up?"

There was a pause while nobody said a word. Everyone listened carefully for any little sound outside. Then Malone broke the silence.

"She is our safe ticket out of here. As long as we hold her life in our hands, they'll be forced to let us go without a fight. We should be able to reach the airstrip without any hassle, and Al keeps a fixed wing fueled and ready at all times. We can be in Baja California inside a matter of hours. I know some people living down there, and it's a good place to live, at least for a while."

"Getting out of the house and into the car ought to be challenging, especially if they've got snipers among their ranks, and we should expect they would. We could be some easy targets the way I see it, guys. Maybe we should make a deal."

"Make a deal?" said Malone, "Michael, if you want to surrender and try to bargain for some kind of reduced prison sentence, go right ahead."

"You mean that, boss?"

"Go ahead. Nobody here is going to stand in your way."

"Maybe it's the only reasonable way out of this."

"Then get on with it, damn it!"

Wendy heard the footsteps across the floor, then the door opening. It didn't close right away.

"Don't worry, boss. I won't give those pigs any information."

"I know you won't, Michael. In fact, I'm certain you won't. You've worked for me for a lot of years. Now get out of here and lock the door behind you before I change my mind."

The door then closed. There was silence in the house, and then shouts were heard outside. Men ordered him face down on the lawn. Then the deafening blast of a handgun being discharged in the house, followed by the light ping of an empty cartridge bouncing on the hardwood floor. Wendy could smell the gunpowder residue.

"He won't be telling them anything at all now," Malone said in a tone of confidence.

"We could cover ourselves and the lady with a blanket and they wouldn't know who to shoot. They wouldn't know which head was the lady's."

"That would probably work," Malone responded, "but moving would be awkward. And then what would we do when we reached the car? I have a better idea. Rick, get me that double-barreled shotgun hanging in the hallway. And while you're at it, bring some bread bag ties from the kitchen."

Again Wendy heard footsteps across the floor. Outside, the police would be formulating their own plan of action. Things were happening fast now. Rick returned a moment later with the items requested.

"It's ten gauge," he said, "but I don't believe there's a single ten gauge shell in the whole house for this old wall hanger."

"That's fine. They don't know we don't have shells. The girl will be gagged, so she can't tell them. With the triggers wired back, my thumb will be the only thing holding those hammers back. If anything were to happen to me, both hammers would automatically fall. They'll be happy to avoid that, since the barrels will be resting against the girl's neck as we leave."

"It's a perfect plan," Rick said.

"I know," bragged Malone, "but if somebody doesn't get that gag back on her soon, we'll never get to test it. Might as well free up her feet at the same time. We're going to take a little walk outside."

Wendy was gagged and lifted to her feet, and the painful ankle ties were removed. Her knees were weak. She wasn't sure if that was from being in the same position for such a long time, or just her nervousness.

A low flying helicopter circled the rooftop, and law enforcement vehicles were collecting along the country road, just outside of pistol range.

"If I'm hit by a bullet, the girl's head gets blown off!" Leo Malone announced in a loud voice so that everyone would hear him as he exited the house with Wendy walking awkwardly in front of him, blindfolded, gagged, and her wrists tied behind her back. He held the shotgun muzzles pressed between her shoulder blades.

"These shotgun triggers are wired to the back of the trigger guard. If my thumb slips off the hammers, she will be a mess. If I see any cops following our car, she gets it. Let us drive away safely, and we'll let her go unharmed when we're in the clear."

The small group moved slowly across the driveway, past the dead man on the front lawn, and Wendy could hear the squelch on a walkie-talkie some distance away. She started feeling dizzy, and she knew that if she got into that car with these wicked killers, she would be dead for certain. There would be snipers in position with their crosshairs on each armed criminal, but they would hold their fire under the present circumstances. If only they knew that shotgun had no shells in it.

She was beginning to feel weak, but she knew what she had to do. Without delaying and possibly missing her only opportunity, she moved swiftly and decisively. She bent forward to allow her hands behind her back to swing up to the shotgun barrels, and she clutched them with a death grip before rotating her body quickly to her left. It was a variation on a martial arts move Trevor taught her several years ago.

Before Malone was able to figure it out and react, the gun barrels were no longer pointed at her, and she could hear shots being fired. It was the last thing she could remember before losing consciousness.

She came to on the lawn near the driveway without the blindfold over her eyes or the gag in her mouth. Her wrists were sore, but her hands were free. Her eyes found Del's face, and she could see the sense of relief in his eyes. An emergency medic was assessing her condition.

"Was I shot?" she asked, nervously inspecting herself.

"No. You just blacked out, that's all. We're taking a look at that area where you hit your head when you fell. It doesn't look too bad. How do you feel?"

"I guess I feel okay. What about those..." she looked across the lawn, "...men?" She saw Leo Malone and his hired gunmen on the front lawn where they fell. Their corpses were photographed and inspected by the forensics people now at the scene. When the officer in charge became aware that Wendy was now conscious, he knelt down on a knee where he could talk to her.

"How are you feeling, Miss Luppert?"

"I think I'll be okay now. Thank you for saving my life. I know they were ready to kill me. When will I be able to go home?"

"Pretty soon, I promise. We've got a few routine procedures. We have to finish our report, but we can contact you later for details. We've got your number," he turned to Del, "Delmar, if you could break away for just a moment, I want to show you something."

Del kissed Wendy on her forehead and then got up and followed the officer. They talked quietly for no more than a few minutes while closely scrutinizing Malone's corpse only twenty feet from where Wendy sat on the lawn. She'd been moved a short distance from where she'd fallen. When Del returned and sat down on the lawn next to Wendy, the medic had already concluded his business and was walking away. She was anxious to find out all that was said.

"Apparently only four shots were fired by law enforcement," he told her in a low voice.

"So? I only see four bodies, besides that first guy Malone killed before we came out of the house," she said, once again glancing over at the bodies on the ground.

"Well, Mr. Malone was hit by two rifle bullets. The Tac snipers used only 5.56mm rifles here, but those forensics people over there are pretty certain that one of Malone's entrance wounds was made by thirty caliber."

She thought for a moment, then flashed Del a serious look, "Trevor?"

Del looked from side to side to make sure nobody was tuning in to their conversation, and then nodded, "You know how precision and thorough he is about everything. He wasn't going to leave your safety entirely in their hands, no matter how good their snipers are. He knows he won't miss a shot with that scoped AR10 .308 of his."

"Do you know where he'll be going now?" she asked, "He can't very well stay around here very much longer, with everything that's happened. Do you think I'll ever get to see him again?"

"Two weeks," he said.

"What? What's going to happen in two weeks?"

"He told me to tell you to check your mailbox in two weeks. That's when you will find the plane ticket to an unnamed destination in the Caribbean. He'll meet you at the airport."

"What if I don't want to go? What if I want to stay here with you?"

"That's impossible."

She looked at him for an explanation, "Impossible?"

"I will already be there, wherever it is. My plane arrives the day before. I think he intends to throw me a bachelor party. My last day as a single man, you know."

Her jaw dropped and her eyes started watering over, "We're going to be…?"

"Does that mean yes?"

"You know it's yes, Delmar Mackenzie. You always knew I would say yes. How could there have ever been any doubt in your mind?"

He shook his head, "You are right. How could I ever doubt it? Even the first time we met, I must have known it somewhere in my mind. That brother of yours made sure it all turned out this way. The ceaseless schemer that he is."

She smiled, "That's Trevor Luppert. Nobody else could have done it all the way he did it."

THE END

Would you like to see your manuscript become a book?

If you are interested in becoming a PublishAmerica author, please submit your manuscript for possible publication to us at:

acquisitions@publishamerica.com

You may also mail in your manuscript to:

**PublishAmerica
PO Box 151
Frederick, MD 21705**

www.publishamerica.com

PUBLISHAMERICA

LaVergne, TN USA
21 January 2011
213409LV00001B/23/P